TIMELESS

A GOTHIC ROMANCE

JAN SCARBROUGH

SADDLE HORSE PRESS

Print ISBN: 978-0-9971920-2-5
1st Digital Release, September 2013
2nd Digital Release, October 2015
1st Print Release July 2017

Edited by Karen Block
Cover Design by The Killion Group Inc.

This edition is published by agreement with Saddle Horse Press,
PO Box 221543, Louisville, KY 40252.

For Dale Epley
who taught me about the metaphysical

TIMELESS

Timeless is a terrific choice for someone looking for a softer romance and who enjoys a Gothic novel in the Barbara Michaels vein.

When Beth Abbott receives a surprise inheritance from her birth mother, she travels to the family's nineteenth century mansion in Old Louisville, now a bed and breakfast. There she meets the resident ghost, a little girl whose crying not only scares, but also intrigues guests. Beth sets out to discover the identity of the ghost and why she appears happy to Beth, not sad.

Jeff Halstead, a man with several secrets, runs the bed and breakfast. But he's more than that to Beth, and she feels their connection immediately. A psychic medium who doubts his skills, Jeff slowly uncovers the truth of their past lives. Will he be in time to reveal the identity of Beth's enemy? Will the love they shared in the past follow them into the future?

CHAPTER ONE

Bowling Green, Kentucky
Present Day

My life changed on a dreary day in December. Oh, the day started out as usual. I made it to work at Eggs-to-Go with six minutes to spare. The seven o'clock starting time has always been hard on me because I'm not a morning person. But I like my waitressing job. I like serving the variety of people who come into the breakfast and brunch restaurant. Many of them are college students because Bowling Green is a college town. Gulping down cups of hot coffee has helped me make it through the longest shifts with a smile.

On the day my life changed, I had a test to study for, so I stopped by the Western Kentucky University library before going home. I can't study in the apartment. Mom is always watching CSPAN or Fox News, and the noise drives me crazy. Mom's a little hard of hearing, so she turns up the volume, you see. The quiet library is better for me. For one thing, studying there makes me feel as if I'm a real college student, not a twenty-five year old, part-time, night school student.

Anyway, I got home late, because I stopped on the way to pick up a quart of skim milk and a carton of peppermint ice cream. It was close enough to Christmas for Mom's favorite ice cream to be in the store. I thought I'd surprise her.

I was the one surprised.

We live in a two-bedroom apartment. Nothing grand. We've lived there together since my dad left us. He's not my real dad—just my adoptive dad—so I don't claim any of his irresponsible genes. When Mom got breast cancer, the jerk declared he couldn't handle it. That left me to take care of Mom when they divorced.

After all, since my mom adopted me as a baby when my birth mother gave me up, I figure I owe her. Oh, sure, I understand her subtle message that I'm her reason for living, especially now that *he's* left us. Being someone's reason for living is a chore. It's not easy carrying someone's happiness on your shoulders. But this had been my way of life for a long time. It was the only life I knew.

Until that day when I unlocked the apartment door and walked into the living room. Sitting beside my mom on one end of the sofa was a balding man with thick, black-framed glasses. He wore a three-piece suit and a red power tie. He looked official, but not particularly powerful. When I walked in carrying the plastic grocery bag, he stood up.

Mom jumped up too, as if she was nervous.

"Beth, this is Mr. Carmichael," she said. "He's from Louisville, and he's come to see you."

He stepped forward and extended his hand, tight lipped, his eyes boring into mine. I took his hand. It was limp and clammy. I didn't think much of him, not with a handshake like that. Shouldn't city lawyers be manlier?

"You look like your mother," he said.

That got my attention, I tell you. I glanced at Mom. We didn't look a bit alike. She's dark haired with an olive complexion. I've always been blond and fair. But then again, we aren't really related. Not by blood anyway.

My gaze shot up to meet the man's black eyes. What had he said? A knot of something like panic tightened in my stomach. I licked my lips. They were suddenly dry.

"Well, sit down, everyone." Mom was flustered. I could tell by the way she pulled her worn sweater around her as if the old blue yarn would protect her from the awkward coldness that filled the room.

I plopped down on the straight-back wooden chair near the writing desk and put the plastic grocery bag on the desktop. I sat bolt upright on the edge of my chair, clenching my teeth together, and folded my hands in my lap. Something was coming, and I felt the raw energy of it. I didn't know if it was good or bad, but from Mom's expression, it couldn't be too bad. She was obviously agitated but not all teary-eyed like the day she learned Grandpa had died.

Mom fidgeted. She smiled and shifted her gaze between us. "Mr. Carmichael has good news for you, Beth."

I lifted my eyebrows, daring the man to say what he'd come to say.

"I am the attorney for the estate of Melissa Chadwick Williams," he said hesitating, as if weighing his words. "Mrs. Williams died of pancreatic cancer two months ago."

I tilted my head to the side as if to ask "So?" What did this have to do with me?

Mr. Carmichael glanced at Mom. "Do you want to tell her, Mrs. Abbott?"

I guess he thought my mom could soften whatever blow was to come, but I'd already figured it out. This woman who'd died was my real mother, and he was her lawyer.

So I saved everyone the trouble. "What do you want with me, Mr. Carmichael? I assume this Mrs. Williams is my birth mother. She's dead. I'm sorry. But what does her passing have to do with me?"

"Everything, Miss Abbott." He cleared his throat. "You see, she left the bulk of her estate, and that of her late husband, to you."

Now I couldn't speak. My mouth dropped open, and then I clamped it shut so I wouldn't look like a goon.

"Beth, it's a lot of money!" Mom's eyes gleamed with excitement, as if we'd just won the Powerball.

"Just how much money is it?"

"In the ballpark of two million dollars in property and investments."

"You're shitting me?"

"Beth, our money worries are over! You won't have to work so hard. You can go to school fulltime!" Mom's voice was breathless, the elation welling up and bursting forth.

I turned to the lawyer. "Look, Mr. Carmichael, my mom and I get by with her monthly disability check and what I make waiting tables, and now you drop out of the blue to tell me I'm a millionaire." I shook my head. "That only happens in movies. How do I know you're telling the truth?"

He pulled official-looking papers out of his briefcase, stood up, and crossed the floor to give them to me. "This is a copy of Melissa's will."

My chest tightened. I accepted the papers and scanned them. What did I know about wills? But I was suspicious enough of this middle-aged guy to turn a skeptical gaze on him. "Why would she leave me her money? She didn't want me when she had me."

I swallowed hard. This was the truth of my birth. Abandoned. Rejected. Not wanted. How many adopted kids felt like me? Although I made the best of the lot God gave me, I'd always thought life had been a little unfair. My adopted parents weren't so bad. They loved me, at least Mom did. I hadn't had such a bad life. Many kids had it harder than me. But I still didn't really belong anywhere.

So why should I now believe life was suddenly going to be rosy when this stranger from Louisville had just made the hurt of my abandonment crawl out from the place I'd stuffed it all these years?

Mr. Carmichael sat down on the sofa. "Melissa was worried about your reaction," he said. "She discovered your whereabouts when you were in high school after her husband died. However, she didn't feel right about coming back into your life."

I leaned back in my chair, smirking, and gazed at the man, not giving an inch. What did he want from me? Was I supposed to jump for joy because this woman who claimed to be my mother had found me and wanted to give me money?

He cleared his throat again. "That changed when she got cancer. She had no other children and neither did her husband. She'd married him in her early twenties when he was already forty-five. They had no immediate family. Melissa wanted to make it right for you. By then, she knew the circumstances of your life."

That a perfect stranger could learn "the circumstances of my life" offended me. But I guess anyone can learn anything about you through the Internet. All you have to do is "Google" a name, and almost instantly you've got a complete rundown on that person. Anyway, I felt defensive. It was my life. It wasn't so bad.

"The cancer took her quickly, within weeks." Mr. Carmichael looked sad. It *was* sad, of course. "She still had time to make her will—to leave you as her heir."

I sat up and forward. "What about my birth father?" That was the big question. Where was that scumbag?

"He was never in the picture. Melissa got pregnant her freshman year at college. Her parents were horrified. They made her come home, but they couldn't make her have an abortion."

Thank goodness for small favors. Was this revelation supposed to make me grateful to this woman? If she'd loved me, she'd have found a way to keep me. Then maybe I wouldn't always be a fish out of water.

"Beth, Mr. Carmichael is the lawyer our lawyer got you from," Mom said to explain, clenching her hands.

I'd heard most of my life that I'd been adopted through a private agreement. My parents had dealt only with their lawyer who brought them the baby. That baby was me, of course, but it had always felt like I had been traded like a horse.

The identities of either party were never revealed to the other lawyer. I understood ours had died soon afterwards and his practice closed. That my birth mother had found me when I'd never sought to be found was a bit mindboggling.

"Let me get this straight." I was hurt and angry by this time, but forced myself to maintain eye contact. "My real father was simply a sperm donor, probably a drunk college kid, and my mother was a college freshman who was stupid enough to get herself knocked up."

"Melissa had never been away from home." Mr. Carmichael was quick to defend his client. "She'd always been under her father's thumb. Let's just say, when she went to college, she sowed her wild oats."

"And then she got cancer and thought she'd right her wrongs. Did she get religion too?"

"Beth!"

I'd crossed the line with my mouth. Glancing at Mom, I clamped it shut and sat back. I hoped my eyes were shooting daggers at the lawyer. I didn't like the guy, and he probably didn't like me either. Or maybe it was the situation he didn't like. After all, he'd been the one to clean up this Melissa's messes too many times.

Mom was pasty white. I guessed I didn't look much better. I felt sick to my stomach and raw. Exposed. As if someone had dragged me up a mountain trail kicking and screaming.

"Melissa regretted her mistake all the days of her life. I know you don't believe it, but she regretted giving you up," the lawyer explained, getting angry himself. "Her parents made her do that too. Let's just say, they didn't want the scandal."

So now I was a mistake and a scandal. Who were her parents anyway? Neanderthals? Didn't they get with the real world? I felt a twinge of sympathy for the teenage mother who'd been my birth mother.

I let out a long breath. "Okay, Mr. Carmichael, I'm sorry about Melissa's hard luck. And it isn't as if we can't use the money. My *real* mother has had cancer too. You can see that we don't have much income." I paused and let out another deep breath. "We will be glad to take the money."

"It's not that simple."

Oh, so there was a catch. How come I didn't guess? Tilting my head away from him, I crossed my arms as if to protect myself.

"But I thought you said my daughter would inherit two million dollars," Mom said in a whiny voice.

"She will, Mrs. Abbott. It's just that the bulk of it is in trust." He nodded toward the will that I had placed on the desk, and then said to my mom, "If you read it carefully, you will see that Beth's money will be managed by a trust until she turns thirty-five. In acknowledgement of your love for Beth, you will receive a monthly stipend from the trust to make your situation easier."

Well, that was something. Maybe Mom wouldn't have to worry so much about making ends meet.

He continued, now staring at me over the rims of his black glasses, "Beth will be expected to move to Louisville and live in the family's bed and breakfast for a year. Melissa wanted her daughter to learn about her family history."

"What?" I didn't like Louisville. It was too big. And I wasn't too fond of change anyway.

"The Chadwick Bed and Breakfast is in the Victorian mansion in Old Louisville that was owned by Melissa's family. You are the last blood relative. The house, the heritage, is yours."

All I could do was mouth "Wow." Now he had my attention. I liked history, and the thought of actually owning a piece of it was pretty cool.

"You'll need to come with me tonight," he said.

"Now? At Christmastime?" My mom's voice rose in anguish. She depended on me after all.

"Yes, those are the conditions of the will."

Something washed over me then. My inherent skepticism took over. This *was* too good to be true. Why should I go with a perfect stranger? I needed time, and he wasn't giving it to me. He could be an ax murderer for all I knew.

I set my jaw. "I can't come tonight or tomorrow. I have a test Wednesday. A final. And I have to do something about my job. I can't walk out on them. And Mom and I need to talk."

Mr. Carmichael stood. He looked stern and foreboding. "You understand that you have no choice if you want the money."

"I understand that's what you tell me." I stood too. "Can I keep this will?"

"Yes. It's a copy." He handed me his card. "Melissa would be pleased you're conscious of your responsibilities. Nevertheless, I expect you in my office Friday at four o'clock, if you want to inherit Mrs. Williams' estate."

I glanced down at the engraved business card. "I'll be there," I told him and looked up.

"It's been a pleasure to meet you, Miss Abbott." He extended his hand, and I took the wet, limp, fish-like hand and gave it my best firm shake. I watched him flinch from the pressure. "I only wish your mother had met you."

I bet she'd have been thrilled. Sarcasm didn't become me, Mom always said. But I saved my manners and didn't say what I thought. I escorted the lawyer the few steps to the door and then closed it firmly behind him.

"Oh, Beth, this is a godsend," Mom said breathlessly.

"I suppose so, but at Christmas? What will you do?"

"I have my church group and the neighbors. He said I'd get some money to live on. I'll be all right."

"But at Christmas, Mom? You'll be lonely."

For the first time in a long while, my mom acted like her old self. She came to me and took my hands, holding them and squeezing them tight. "I know you don't like to take risks, Beth, but you're an old soul. You'll be okay. This is something you've got to do. Sure, the money will be good, but more than that, this is a way to find out about yourself. Who you really are is the one thing your dad and I couldn't give you."

I looked into her soft brown eyes. This woman didn't give me life, but she'd given me something more—her love and understanding. She knew, even more than I knew that this opportunity was important. More than the money, it was about my identity. And the deep, dark sadness and shame I'd carried with me since the day I was born.

CHAPTER TWO

After we hugged, Mom disappeared into her bedroom where I heard her calling her sister. I opened my laptop and did a quick Google search. Mr. Carmichael's name showed up on the Kentucky Bar Association website, so he was telling the truth about being a lawyer. His address on the site matched the address on his business card.

That settled, I next searched for the Chadwick Bed and Breakfast and found a website for it that told me "the original home was built by a millionaire tycoon in the style of the Georgian Revival, faithfully reproducing the lines and colors of an Italian Renaissance palazzo in traditional Florentine architecture." *Good grief!* That was certainly ostentatious.

The house was massive. Viewing the pages on the website, I counted seven guest rooms used for the bed and breakfast. And the "millionaire tycoon" who built the place in the 1880s impressed me. Thomas Chadwick made his money in dry goods, railroads, utilities and banking. Was he my great-grandfather, however many greats back?

In the blink of an eye, I'd gone from no real history to belonging to a famous Kentucky family. It was hard for me to wrap my arms around the idea. After all, in my mind I remained the same Beth Abbott, adopted child, waitress, and sometime college student who had always been unlucky in love. Not much glory in that description, or in my life up to this point, anyway.

When Mom emerged from her bedroom, she was aglow. "It's settled," she announced happily. "Mary Beth is picking me up and taking me to St. Louis to visit during Christmas. I may stay a few months with her. I don't know yet."

"That's great, Mom! You won't be alone for the holiday." I'd been named "Elizabeth" for my aunt, and she'd always been a role model for me. Independent. Strong. Successful. All the things I hadn't managed to be quite yet.

"It won't stop me worrying about you though," Mom said, "but I figure if you don't need to worry about me, you'll find your new life easier."

Her sacrifice brought tears to my eyes, but I swiped them away and then showed the website for the Chadwick house. We spent an hour scrolling through each page, studying the fancy rooms. It was a good time, sort of a parting of the ways for us. My mom had finally stopped depending on me and reached out to her sister. I was going on an adventure, albeit one not of my own making, but I told myself I would not be scared. I could handle this change. After all, I was by rights, a Chadwick.

I took my Basic Marketing Concepts final on Wednesday and passed it with flying colors. Mom insisted that I go to the Sears store at the Greenwood Mall and buy new luggage. She didn't want me to look like a poor relation when I arrived in Louisville. I bought a travel bag on wheels for my laptop and a three-piece set that included two suitcases on wheels of different sizes, and a shoulder bag.

The thought of packing my whole life into four pieces of luggage was a bit daunting, but Mom helped me wash and press my clothes. She also made me take my Madame Alexander baby doll I'd had since I was a kid. I called her Victoria. She had blue eyes and blond hair with bangs and pigtails tied with blue gingham bows. Her pink dress had puffed sleeves and plenty of ruffles on the bodice. She wore white patent leather Mary Jane's with pink bows. Mom had given me the doll for my eighth birthday, when times were good and we all were happy.

Was it silly to take my doll? After all I was an adult now, not a kid. Mom said it was a connection with my past, and I should think of her when I looked at Victoria.

On Friday morning, I started out my adventure. I drove our only car, a used Honda Civic that got good gas mileage and was still in pretty good shape. Mom didn't shed a tear, not in my presence anyway. We're troopers, she told me, giving me a tight hug. I don't know how I made it to I-65, because there were tears in my eyes, blurring my vision. But I was underway and soon overcame my sadness at leaving home.

The gnawing fear in my stomach was more difficult to squelch. This was a risk, after all, and I had learned to be cautious after making dumb-headed mistakes as a teenager when I was trying to please a boy. Like the time a bunch of us drove to Florida in a "borrowed" car and were arrested for drinking. I was underage and my record expunged; however, my parents had spent a fortune flying me home to Kentucky.

Mr. Carmichael's office in Louisville was in a very tall building on Market Street. I finally found it, but only after crossing the interstate bridge over the Ohio River into Indiana by mistake. I stopped at a gas station, and the clerk directed me to the Second Street Bridge. I crossed back over the river into Kentucky and was able to find the big building after that and make it into the underground parking garage. Did I tell you I hate big cities like Louisville?

Mr. Carmichael was late for the appointment. He's a lawyer, after all. So I stood at the window of his waiting room, twenty-four stories up in the air and gazed toward the Ohio River. I could see the big clock on the Indiana side, the bridges, and the Falls of the Ohio. It was a bright day with plenty of sunshine and blue sky. For some reason, I felt as if the town was welcoming me.

"Miss Abbott, I'm glad to see you," Mr. Carmichael said, breezing through the office door. "I'm sorry I'm late."

I turned to view the man's flustered features. His arms were full of papers and binders, and he looked disheveled, not like the cool, collected man from my apartment living room. He explained he'd been in a difficult deposition and invited me into his office.

We sat across a huge wooden desk from each other. The light from the window behind him gave his bald head a sort of halo appearance. I wondered if he was my guardian angel or something, for he certainly had brought me life-changing news earlier in the week.

I reserved judgment about whether it was good news.

"So you're here to fulfill the terms of the will," he stated flatly.

I nodded. "I've come as instructed."

He seemed pleased. "I have a check for your mother, as we discussed. Do you want me to mail it to your apartment in Bowling Green?"

I told him my aunt's address and watched him write it down. He called his secretary into the office and handed the address and check to her. When she was gone, he settled back into his office chair and regarded me over the rims of his glasses.

"Do you have any questions for me?"

I was nervous, the pit of my stomach turning cartwheels. I clasped my hands together in my lap. "What exactly am I supposed to do for a year? How am I supposed to learn about my family, which, I take it, is the condition of my birth mother's will?"

I couldn't call her "mother" outright. Heck, I didn't even know what the woman had looked like. She didn't seem real at all to me.

"That's an astute question." Mr. Carmichael cleared his throat.

"The bed and breakfast is run, expertly I must say, by a man named Jeff Halstead. He manages the property and is the chef for the morning breakfasts. He's been there since 2002. If you want to learn the business, he can teach you."

"I'm sure he won't take kindly to my interference," I said, "especially if he's been employed there so long."

"Jeff is more than an employee. He was Melissa's nephew by marriage. But since her husband was older when they married, she and Jeff were about the same age. He took her death hard."

Great. Another reason he'd view me as an interloper. I let out a breath. "I still don't understand what I'm supposed to do. How do I learn about the family?"

"Melissa felt that living in the house would bring you closer to your family history. There are albums of old photographs and books in the library. You can make yourself useful to Jeff in some way. You are a waitress, aren't you?"

His reference to my means of employment raised my hackles. "I like waitressing," I stated bluntly. "Do you have any objection if I enroll in college? I understand the University of Louisville campus is nearby."

"That's a wonderful idea. I'm sure Melissa would have approved."

I resisted the urge to roll my eyes. I'd spent my life so far trying to please one mother and now was going to please the one I didn't know and would never have the opportunity to meet.

We talked business then. Mr. Carmichael gave me a checkbook with a debit card and access to a bank account. He made it clear he'd be watching my spending for the first year. In other words, the money wasn't mine yet, but he didn't want me to be without funds while in Louisville.

I did appreciate that bit of thoughtfulness. Without the bank account, I'd be forced to wait tables again to earn spending money. This way I was free of that burden and could focus on my new duty to learn about my family, a notion I was beginning to embrace.

He took me to an early dinner at a fancy restaurant called Vincenzo's, which was within walking distance of his office building. We returned to his building after dark. The December day had turned chilly. I shook his hand in parting.

"Jeff is expecting you," he said. "Just ring the front doorbell. He'll get you situated."

I thanked him and headed to my car. All I had to do was leave the garage, turn right and then right again on Third Street. The house was on Third Street. I had memorized the number.

When the business district turned residential, Christmas lights sparkled from front porches and windows. Old Louisville appeared festive enough, even though bare, skeletal tree branches quivered in the wind, lending an eerie feeling to my drive. I found the house number and parked on the street in front of the imposing, three-storied structure that was the Chadwick Bed and Breakfast. Colored lights twinkled in the bushes that flanked the stone steps and a single electric candle flickered in each window that faced the street.

Climbing out of the car, I removed my laptop case, shoulder bag, and the smallest wheeled suitcase from the trunk. Then I made my way up the front walk to the huge porch, or portico, since the Victorian home was patterned after Italian Renaissance architecture. Twelve Ionic columns, the kind with the scrolls at the top, held the roof of the portico.

I paused at the ornate wooden front door to catch my breath, letting go of the handles of the wheeled bags. More than afraid, I experienced an odd feeling. I was embarking on an unknown journey. A huge risk. Now that I saw the house, my change of circumstances became an actuality, and the importance of the moment settled on my shoulders like a heavy burden.

I rang the doorbell and waited.

The door opened. The light glowing from the inside revealed a tall man wearing black shoes and jeans, a white turtleneck, and an open, red cotton cardigan sweater with a zipper down the front. His hair was jet back, and so were his long eyelashes that fringed blue eyes. His dark eyebrows furrowed as he gazed at me, and his eyes lit with recognition. My skin prickled because of a chill that had nothing to do with the December night.

"You're Melissa's daughter," he said in a deep baritone voice.

I swallowed, looking up at him and, because of our age difference, felt very much like a misbehaving child. "Yes," I said.

He stepped aside without a word so that I could enter. I grabbed the handles of my two wheeled bags and stumbled across the threshold into a wonderland of lights and magic.

The massive entrance hall with beamed ceilings and a crystal chandelier seemed like an English castle to me. Doors opened off the hall and I caught glimpses of lavish furniture and paintings, all antique, I supposed. A grand staircase, also impressive with its dark wood railings, led to the floors above. A live Christmas tree stood beside the stairwell, bright and festive and smelling of pine. We'd never had a real Christmas tree, and it caught my attention as much as anything in the room.

"I'm Jeff Halstead," he said, offering me his hand.

I took his hand and immediately at his touch, an odd feeling of euphoria swept over me. His handshake was strong, decisive, unlike the wet-fish handshake of Mr. Carmichael. I gazed up into his eyes and experienced a compelling sense of awareness.

My tongue felt tangled. "This is awkward for me, Mr. Halstead."

"Jeff," he noted and dropped my hand, taking a step back from me. "Set your luggage by the staircase, and let me take your coat. I'll show you around."

I parked my luggage near the first step and turned to face him. He seemed familiar to me, but I knew I'd never seen him before.

He'd known me right away, of course. Perhaps I did look like my birth mother. Or did he just make the assumption based upon Mr. Carmichael's instructions?

I unbuttoned my winter coat and shrugged it off as he helped me remove it. The act seemed so intimate and only added to my sense of the familiarity about him. He faltered, as if he too detected something strange, but collected himself with a stiffening of his posture and turned to hang the coat on an antique coat rack in the corner.

"The first room is the ladies parlor or morning room," he explained, looking down at me and then away. "It is decorated in the style of Louis XVI, and named for the nineteenth century custom of calling on neighbors early in the morning."

I stuck my head in the front parlor room, overwhelmed by a deep sense of déjà vu. It did remind me of the French, all white and gold with antique settees and a tall mirror over the dainty fireplace. The ceiling was high and the tall windows were draped with white sheers and heavy green drapery. It wasn't to my liking, too elaborate for my everyday taste.

On the other side of the hall was the drawing room. It reminded me of a room in an English manor. It was more masculine with red drapes and a striped sofa. A huge painting of seventeenth century women with their flowing gowns hung over the mantle. A baby grand piano nestled quite nicely in one corner. I was to discover that every room was crowded with antiques, gorgeous pieces of crystal or silver, and ornate pictures and mirrors. It was like a Victorian museum. And all this belonged to me.

Or it would someday.

At that thought, I glanced at Jeff, and he was watching my reaction to the room with his mesmerizing eyes. I shivered at his stare, drawn to him by an unfathomable tie that frightened me.

"It's very nice," I said, wondering what he expected of me.

He turned abruptly and walked out of the room. "Down the hall we have the dining room and on the other side of the hall is the library."

I followed, passing the pungent-smelling Christmas tree, and peeked into the dining room and then the library. It was my favorite room with its wood paneling and floor-to-ceiling shelves of old books.

At the end of the hall was a closed door. We paused at it.

"I tell my guests that the only rule of the house is that if a door is closed, then it's off-limits," he said with a forewarning look. "We have seven guest rooms upstairs, some of them suites and all with en suite bathrooms." I frowned a little, and he added, "That means private bathrooms."

"Of course." Gosh, he must think me a real hick.

His face was stoic, almost spooky-like. It wasn't an ugly face. In fact, he was quite handsome. Maybe that was my problem with him. Maybe I was drawn to him in a sexual manner. He had to be in his forties, much too old for me, so I tried to suppress my reaction to him. My female hormones might be in overdrive, but it wasn't a good time to do something stupid.

I'd been stupid so many times before with one boyfriend after another. My track record with men was horrible with every relationship ending after only a few months. Mom often despaired of me saying I'd never get married. But I could never marry a guy who treated me with no respect. For some reason, I always picked jerks to date, like the one who slept with my girlfriend while trying to get into *my* pants.

"I'll show you the back end of the house, the non-public area, now," Jeff continued. "You'll need to know it, if you want to run the bed and breakfast eventually."

He opened the closed door that led to another, less elegant hallway. On the side of the room nearest to the dining room was a modern kitchen with stainless steel appliances like you'd see on

HGTV. There was a smaller dining room behind it where the staff had once dined. I thought of *Downton Abbey*, the PBS show Mom and I enjoyed watching. When this house was built, it must have had servants like those in the show. That fascinated me and spiked my interest in the history of the house *and* the family. *My family.* It wasn't just my mother that drew my curiosity. I wondered about the life she'd come from. The life her father and his father must have led.

At the end of the hall was another closed door. Jeff explained that it led to the outside courtyard. "I live in the converted carriage house on the other side of the courtyard. After Melissa's husband died, she moved in upstairs over my apartment."

That caught my interest too. He must have seen the speculation in my eyes, for he frowned again. A deep, forbidding frown.

"Melissa was my aunt by marriage," he said in a measured voice, making sure I knew there was nothing romantic between them.

"I know. Mr. Carmichael told me."

He shoved his fingers through that rumpled head of black hair and turned quickly.

"Would you like something to eat? A cup of coffee, maybe?"

I shook my head no. "Mr. Carmichael fed me."

"Then I will show you upstairs to your room for tonight."

I followed him like a loyal puppy. He had a hitch in his stride, almost as if he was favoring an old injury. Somehow that made him more romantic and mysterious. I smiled at the thought, but determined not to go there.

"We've had a cancellation, so I'll show you to the Derby Room," he stated. "Tomorrow you can decide if you'd rather stay in Melissa's old rooms. They will be more private."

"Okay," I muttered, wondering what was in store for me.

He grabbed the handles of my wheeled luggage and started up

the staircase. I slung the carryall bag over my shoulder and headed upstairs behind him.

"Only two of our rooms are occupied tonight." He glanced behind his shoulder as if to gauge my reaction. "Tomorrow night we have booked the dining room for a catered party. All guests will have left by then, because we are closed Christmas Eve and Christmas Day."

Christmas was on Monday, so that meant Sunday and Monday there would be no one in this house but the two of us.

I swallowed hard at the thought, more so because of the awkwardness of this whole situation, not simply because he was attractive and enigmatic. Or because I feared the strange connection I felt toward him.

"Do you visit family at Christmas, Mr. 'er Jeff?" I caught myself before calling him Mr. Halstead.

"I have no family since Melissa's death."

"Oh." That sounded sad. At least I had my mom.

"What about you? Will you be going back to Bowling Green?"

I shook my head, but he couldn't see it because I was still behind him as we walked down the second floor hall. "No, my mom has gone to visit her sister."

"I see."

Was he realizing that it would just be the two of us? I knew no one in Louisville. It wasn't as if I had anyone to visit or a place to go.

He stopped at a shut door and turned the doorknob. Flicking on the overhead lights, he entered the room with me on his tail. "We have cable TV and Wi-Fi," he said. "There should be clean towels and everything you need in the bathroom."

I walked inside and turned in circles to stare at the room. "Thanks."

"Breakfast is served from seven in the morning until ten," he told me. "Unless you can think of something you need, I'll leave you to settle in."

I faced him. There was a stiff formality about him—an aloofness. Maybe that is why I thought him strange. But there was something about his eyes, the way he looked at me that caused me to feel more than just a sexual attraction. A cold chill went through my body.

"I'll see you then," I said and wished him goodnight.

"Good night, Beth," he whispered and backed through the doorway.

The door swung shut silently. I shivered. That was the first time he'd called me by my name. I didn't even know he knew my name, but of course, he did. Like Mr. Carmichael, he probably knew everything about me.

Yet, I knew nothing about him. And more than anything, I wanted to find out more.

CHAPTER THREE

The Derby Room was more than a room: it was a suite with a parlor and a separate bedroom and bath. Just as in the rooms downstairs, the sitting room was crammed with antiques—a vintage empire sofa, Victorian wingback chairs and a writing desk. I wandered into the second room, flipping the light switch that turned on ornate wall sconces. A king-size canopy bed dominated the room. The private tile and marble bath contained a deep Victorian claw-foot bathtub that had been fitted with a shower.

I pulled my luggage into the bedroom. It was only seven-thirty and although I was tired from the day, I wasn't sleepy. Opening the doors to an antique armoire, I discovered a flat screen TV. I turned it on and taking the remote, sat on the edge of the big bed under the canopy and flipped channels.

These antique rooms creeped me out. They seemed cold and uninviting, sort of like the much too good-looking innkeeper who had ushered me into them. If this was my family history, I really wanted no part of it. Mom was right. I wasn't a risk-taker. The reality of the adventure was too much for me at the moment. I was suddenly lonesome and homesick. Was it really worth it?

I didn't really belong here, did I?

Leaving the TV on ESPN for company, I went into the bathroom to get ready for bed. After soaking ten minutes in the hot water of the claw-foot bathtub, I put on my flannel pajamas and a pair of socks. I climbed into bed, bringing my laptop with me. Connecting to the Internet, I checked Facebook and Twitter while the TV glowed in the background. Then I surfed, looking for more information on the Chadwick Bed and Breakfast, something more than just their website. I didn't have much luck and at nine-thirty decided to go to sleep.

I went back into the parlor to make sure the door to the hall was locked and turned off the overhead chandelier. On a whim I pulled my Madame Alexander baby doll from the suitcase and propped her on the far side of the bed on the pillow. A doll named Victoria seemed to go perfectly in this old-fashioned setting. Besides, she brought a little reminder of home with her, and as my mom had asked, I thought about her, hoping she was enjoying her visit with her sister.

I turned out the lights and crawled into bed, snuggling down under the elaborate brocade bedspread. Thank goodness there was a fuzzy blanket beneath it that was warm and cozy. I settled in, on my back, and gazed up at the canopy over my head. The bed was so large I felt lost in it. Maybe that's why sleep eluded me. Or maybe it was because I felt I shouldn't be in this room. I sighed and turned on my side to stare at the window illuminated by streetlights below.

It wasn't long before a strange feeling stole over me. Someone was watching. I trembled slightly and turned over on my back. I'd never felt so alone in my life. But then again, it seemed as if I wasn't alone. Turning on the bedside lamp, I jumped out of bed and patrolled the room, even opening the door and looking into the parlor. *Nothing. No one.*

So I clicked off the light, scrambled into bed and pulled the fuzzy blanket up over my head, letting only my nose stick out from under the covers. This was just a new experience. I was away from home. I was nervous anyway. I told myself all these things trying to convince myself that the sensation of being watched was simply my imagination.

I tried to go to sleep. My new life would be better in daylight. I could at least get a better look at my surroundings. Falling asleep would make the day come sooner.

But it didn't work. Even though my eyes were shut tight, I couldn't relax. Time went by. I don't know how much time. And then I heard a faint noise.

It was the giggling of a child.

Could it be television from someone's room?

But it didn't sound like television. It sounded real, as if a child was playing in the hall maybe. It was a high-pitched laugh, like a little girl. My skin prickled, and my stomach tightened. Another chilly sensation swept over me. I was being watched. But there was no one in my room with me.

Tossing back the covers, I jumped out of bed and ran to the nearby window. Could the sound be coming from outside? A streetlamp pooled light on the sidewalk. Gray fog swirled in the air making the deserted street below seem spooky as if from a B-rated horror movie. I shivered at the thought and turned to hop back into bed.

At that moment, a flash of white raced past me, and I caught it out of the corner of my eye. I heard the giggling again, louder now. Looking back at my bed, I spotted a little girl standing on the other side of it. She was dressed in white and her slender hand reached toward my doll as if she wanted to touch it and play with it.

"Hey!"

She looked up, startled, and smiled at me as if she knew me. And then she ran from the bed toward the door to the parlor, which was shut. My heart raced. I followed her, flinging open the door to stare out into the empty parlor with the gray streetlights creating a defused, half-light glow in the room.

How had the little girl gone through the door? It had been shut! How could she have disappeared so quickly? Was I dreaming? Hallucinating? I pinched myself to see if I was awake.

I was. The floor was cold even through my socks. I crossed the parlor and unlocked and opened the outer door to the hall. All was quiet except for the deep tick-tock of a grandfather clock at one end. I bit my lower lip and retreated to the parlor, making sure the door to the hall was locked.

Standing silently for a moment, listening for laughter, I let my heart settle into a normal rhythm. What was the matter with me?

Thinking back at the vision of the little girl, I realized something was wrong about it. The child's clothes were more fitting for the nineteenth century, not the twenty-first. In fact, her clothes reminded me of the lacy frills of my doll. And the girl's hair was long, curled in dark blond ringlets down her back, and she wore a white ribbon in her hair. Her body didn't seem solid. It was transparent, almost ghost-like.

Ah, shit!

I charged back into the bedroom and leaped into the bed, pulling the covers over my head. As if hiding under covers could save me. I was behaving like a child myself, but I didn't know what else to do. I didn't know a phone number to call unless I punched 911. Then what would I say to the firemen or police? I saw a ghost standing by my bed. *Right.* That made as much sense as me inheriting a million dollars from a woman I'd never known or seen.

But I *had* inherited a million dollars...two million to be exact.

That realization didn't thrill me. So I tried to think of another explanation, something besides the paranormal.

Try as I might, I couldn't make sense of my experience. My mind whirled and twirled but I couldn't come up with a clear explanation. Later I heard the grandfather clock bong once in the distance, ghost-like itself. This place was too darn spooky for me, I remember thinking. Soon after that I must have relaxed enough to fall asleep.

———

When I awoke, bright sunshine streamed through the bedroom window. I uncurled from the fetal position I found myself sleeping in and crawled out of bed. Nothing looked out of place. But I was glad to see the sunshine. I felt as if I could make a better connection with this room in the broad daylight. Picking up my cell phone, I checked the time. It was ten-thirty. I'd never slept that late in my life.

And I had missed breakfast.

Well, it couldn't be helped. I hastily dressed in blue jeans, sweater and the cutest tan, ankle-high shoes that looked like cowboy boots under the jeans. The hall outside my room was gloomy and quiet. Too gloomy and too empty. Déjà vu washed over me. I slowly went down the wood-paneled stairs with the thick, dark bannisters, touching the slick surface of the handrails for added security.

The front rooms were empty too, but the door stood open to the back hall. I went through the open door and into the bright kitchen that seemed cozier in the light of day. A woman stood at the sink with her back to me.

"Hello," I said.

She turned around, and I saw that she was real enough with short, spiked hair and a row full of earrings in one ear. I guessed she was my age or younger.

"I'm Beth Abbott," I introduced myself. "I must have missed breakfast."

"Jeff said you might," she replied. "Have a seat. I've kept a plate warm for you."

There was a butcher-block-topped island with four stools pushed up on one side. Pots and pans hung above the island on a metal rack. I climbed aboard one of the stools and propped the soles of my ankle boots on the rungs. Placing my elbows on the island and leaning forward, I surveyed the girl who was busying herself with my breakfast.

"I'm Corey Brooks, by the way," she said when she put a steaming plate of eggs, bacon and grits in front of me. She then brought a plateful of blueberry muffins and served me coffee and orange juice.

I was hungry and told her so when I thanked her. She grinned at me, brought a cup of coffee, and sat down beside me.

"I know you are Mrs. Williams' daughter," she said.

I shrugged. "That's what I'm told." I glanced at her as I buttered a muffin. "It's all very weird to me."

I munched on the muffin, and because she was quiet, studying me, I tried to make conversation. "I guess you work here."

She nodded. "Mrs. Williams helped tutor me at the Cabbage Patch Settlement House where I'd go after school before my mom got home. When I graduated high school, Mrs. Williams asked if I wanted to work here and go to school too. So, I clean rooms and help with breakfast and I go to U of L. She was wonderful to me. She paid my tuition all four years. I'm a senior. I'll graduate in May."

I felt like I had a potential ally. We seemed to have a lot in common. I told her about taking classes at Western and waiting tables. Corey's mother was divorced too, so we could relate in that way.

"I must admit I'm out of my element here," I told her. "I don't know what I'm supposed to do. It's all very unreal."

"I can imagine. But I wish I had someone to give me a lot of money."

It was my turn to shrug. "It's in some sort of trust. I just get an allowance."

She sipped her coffee, and I sipped mine. Smiling at her, I hoped we could be friends.

"Did you cook the breakfast? It's very good."

"No. Jeff did that."

Jeff, the enigmatic man from last night, the guy who attracted me in a strange sort of way. "He's very good looking," I murmured.

Corey's eyebrows lifted, and she grinned. "Don't go getting any ideas. He's a saint or something. Never goes out. Never dates. It's almost as if he doesn't care about women."

"Oh?"

"You can bet I tried when I first came to work here." She nodded her head sheepishly. "Didn't do a bit of good."

Well, now I was warned. Best play it cool anyway. From living with my often-explosive father, to my failure with men, I'd learned it wasn't safe to show what I feel. Plus I didn't need any trouble here, especially when I'd already imagined I'd seen a ghost in my room.

Corey jumped up, picked up the coffee pot, and filled my cup. I poured cream into it and stirred.

"Can I get you anything else?" she offered.

"Oh, no. Thank you, very much. This was perfect."

She removed the plate. "You must have slept well last night," Corey commented casually.

I glanced at her over the rim of my coffee cup. "It was okay once I fell asleep."

"That's good. I guess you didn't see our resident ghost."

"Ghost?" I almost choked on the hot coffee.

She turned back to me with a knowing look. "Yes, a little girl, dressed in white. Several guests have seen her. That's why we're on the Old Louisville Ghost Tour."

"We are?" I could hardly speak.

"It's a great business draw Mrs. Williams always said. She said the little girl used to live here. Long ago."

I set down my coffee cup. My heart beat triple time. I wasn't about to admit seeing the ghost and being scared. But at least I knew I wasn't crazy.

"What happened to the little girl?" I asked, suddenly curious and frightened at the same time.

Corey crept nearer to me as if she enjoyed being the storyteller. Her voice was hushed. "They say she was killed in a tornado."

CHAPTER FOUR

Louisville had been wiped out in a tornado? When? I loved obscure historical details, but before I could react to Corey's revelation about the ghost, a new guy sauntered into the kitchen. He was buff. I could tell because he wore a tight navy sweater that clung to the muscles of his shoulders, chest and arms. His jeans were tight and looked new, as if he took care about his appearance. And he had a cocky way of walking. Even before he came over to Corey and kissed her on the back of the neck, I didn't like him. There was a nervous energy around him. A lot of negativity. He looked just like the guys I usually chose to date.

"Hi, gorgeous," he said.

"Hi, yourself." Corey shrugged him off. "You better behave."

"Ah, c'mon, Corey. I'm just havin' a little fun."

"I've warned you, Eric." Corey turned and looked at me. "Especially now when your new employer is watching. Lay off."

The young kid spun around to stare at me. His eyes widened as if doing a double take. "Well, I'll be damned," he said, the pitch of his voice rising.

"You may be," Corey shot back. "Damned, I mean. But you'd better watch your language. This is Mrs. Williams' daughter."

"Ah, the love child."

I'd never been called that. I had always been the treasured, and loved, adopted daughter. No one had ever referred to my parentage that way until this punk, who was evidently in my employ, said those words to me.

"And you are?" I carefully controlled my voice trying to sound frosty.

He crossed over to the island where I sat. "I'm Eric Hubert," he said resting his elbows on the countertop and leaning toward me. "You're kinda cute."

"For a bastard," I snarled hoping the word would have some shock value.

It did. "Sorry about that. I meant no harm."

Deciding to let it go, I bent toward him and glared. He smelled of cigarette smoke. "And what do you do around here, Mr. Hubert?"

He grinned, a smug, sure-of-himself grin. "Just about anything Jeff wants doing. Gardening, fixing, handyman work." He winked at me. "I'm good at a lot of things."

"I bet you are," I said slowly, not breaking his gaze.

"Don't you have something to do?" Corey shifted her feet as if she was uncomfortable with the whole situation.

I was too. In fact, my stomach was rock hard. I wanted to jump up and run away from the kitchen, but I held my ground, not letting on that I was scared out of my mind. It was a dumb reaction. The kid *was* a punk. He repulsed me. Yet, for a long time, I'd schooled myself never to betray my feelings, especially fear. I wasn't about to let on to this guy the way he affected me.

Eric straightened up slowly, deliberately, never removing his gaze from mine. 'Gotta get the dining room ready for tonight," he said without looking away.

"Then you'd best get at it," Corey commanded from her spot at the kitchen sink.

He blew me a kiss, turned on his heel and strolled out the door. "See you girls later."

"Creep." Corey shuddered, as if to rid herself of his presence.

I felt like doing the same thing, but instead stood and carried my dishes to the sink.

Corey rushed through the cleanup, saying she needed to make up the three bedrooms used last night before the caterers arrived. I offered to help. After all, wasn't that what I was supposed to do? Learn the business?

And I had nothing better to do, did I?

We worked together well, laughing and cutting up. I really had found a friend, I thought. And besides, I liked the work. It seemed so natural to me and comfortable. I liked to see the results when the rooms were clean, the beds made, and the bathtubs sparkled.

In my own room, I bundled up my belongings so that I could move them if and when I was invited. I didn't want to sleep in that king-size bed with its resident ghost another night. Of course, I didn't let on to Corey I'd seen the ghost. Being new here, it seemed like I should keep it my secret.

We were shutting the door to the last bedroom when a voice boomed at us. "What are you doing?"

I turned to see Jeff Halstead surveying us as if we'd stolen the queen's jewels. In the light of day, he was even more darkly good-looking than I'd realized. His eyes were piercing blue, and they seemed to bore right into mine.

Once again I felt that odd connection, tying us together as if some unspoken rope bound us.

"Just finishing up," Mr. Halstead," Corey said in a timid voice.

"I can see that, Corey," he said with a glance of irritation. "I was asking what Miss Abbott was doing."

I carried the vacuum cleaner, so I set it down and stood up, stiffening my back. "I'm helping Corey, Jeff. Doesn't that look like what I'm doing?"

"This is Corey's job."

I couldn't understand the harm and told him so. "Besides, I thought I was supposed to learn about this house and the family."

"Not this way." He was gruff, like a disapproving college professor. "Now gather your suitcases, and I'll take you to your rooms in the carriage house."

I felt like snapping to attention and saluting "Yes, sir," but of course I didn't. I wasn't comfortable challenging him any more than I already had.

Jeff took my suitcase when I pulled it out of the bedroom, so that I only had my laptop case and shoulder bag to handle. Like last night, I trailed behind him, laptop case bumping down the staircase and through the entrance hall. Eric was in the dining room setting up tables when we walked by.

Outside, the air was cold, but the day sunny. I'd forgotten my coat but didn't have time to linger in the brick-paved courtyard to feel the cold. Jeff whisked me across it and through the side door of the garage.

"At one time this building housed the family carriages and stabled its horses. We converted it into a three-car garage and two apartments in the second part of the old barn area." He paused at a shelf and removed a garage door opener device. He handed it to me. "Here. This is yours now. I'd pull your car off the street today. We're expecting snow tomorrow night."

Then Jeff led me out the back door to a covered corridor that separated the two sections of the building. Steps led to a second floor and one end was open to the courtyard.

I glanced toward the house. "Snow?" There wasn't a cloud in the sky.

"I'm just telling you what our notoriously-wrong weathermen say." He gave me a long onceover, his eyes softening.

I wondered at the way he looked at me. What was he thinking? Did he approve of me? Did Melissa disinherit him in favor of me?

"Maybe we'll have a white Christmas, after all," I said not wishing to reveal my true thoughts.

We climbed the stairs to Melissa's apartment. I watched the hitch in Jeff's step and wondered about it. At the top of the staircase were a tiny landing and a door. Jeff used a key to open it. He flicked on the overhead lights and went in ahead of me.

I found that I was holding my breath. There was a slight flutter in my stomach. I crossed the threshold and released that breath, strongly aware of my surroundings. This was where my mother had lived. My birth mother and benefactor. I felt at once hopeful. The living room was nothing like the ones in the big house. It was open and airy with a huge maroon, corduroy sofa and sturdy coffee and end tables. I did a pirouette trying to take in everything. There was too much to see at once. Too much to comprehend.

Yet, I immediately felt at home here. As if I belonged. The room was warm and comfortable and charming. For the first time, I was glad I'd come.

"This is lovely," I said breathlessly.

"Melissa had quiet, simple taste," Jeff responded, his voice deep and earnest.

Glancing around, I could see that what Jeff said was true.

"The layout is a simple, open concept," he continued, walking to the end of the living room where a bar separated it from the kitchen. He turned on the lights in the kitchen. It was modern with stainless steel appliances.

"Melissa took most of her meals with me or the guests. You can do the same, but you can cook if you want." He turned to face me. "It's up to you."

I caught his gaze. "Yes, thank you." I felt my cheeks warm and couldn't think of anything to say.

We stared at each other for a long moment, my beating heart growing loud in my ears, until I finally broke eye contact and looked away.

He took that as a signal to continue his tour. "There is a large bedroom with a king size bed."

Another one of *those*, I thought, thinking once more of that white apparition standing beside the big antique bed last night.

Jeff opened the bedroom door and showed me inside. The colors here were girly colors, deep mauves and pinks, a red throw pillow here and there. At the window overlooking the courtyard enclosed by white plantation shutters, I spotted a wooden desk. The other side of the room opened into a huge modern bathroom with an enormous walk-in closet. Pure heaven for an orphan child from a divorced family, wasn't it?

Coming back into the bedroom from examining the whirlpool tub, I glanced at Jeff and smiled for maybe the first time. "Thank you," I said from the heart. "This is nice. I will like it here."

He frowned. *Why?* At my words or my smile. He seemed uncomfortable, shifting his stance and clearing his throat. "Not my doing. This is all Melissa."

"I wish I'd met her." The words came out of my mouth unexpectedly, but I realized I was sincere.

Digging into a pants pocket, Jeff pulled out a set of keys. "These are to the apartment and the mansion. You may find a key to Melissa's desk. I suspect she's left a note or two for you to find."

He dropped the keys into the palm of my hand. We were close —knee touching close. The energy he emitted soothed me, even in my own state of unease at his nearness. I glanced once again into his blue eyes.

"How do you know?"

He shrugged and turned away, going back into the living room. "I know Melissa. She felt guilty for giving you up. She wanted to make it up to you. She wanted to explain."

Turning again, Jeff confronted me with a serious gaze. "More than anything, she wanted your forgiveness," he said quietly.

"Forgiveness," I mouthed almost in a whisper, suddenly going cold.

At that moment, I understood that I needed forgiveness too. I needed to be pardoned for hating my birth mother all these years.

CHAPTER FIVE

Jeff shut the door behind him, leaving me at loose ends alone in the living room. What should I do next? After a moment, I wheeled my luggage into the bedroom and dropped the shoulder bag on the pink bedspread. I should unpack, settle in, but I wanted to bring in my big suitcase before starting. So fishing my wallet with my driver's license in it and my car keys out of my purse, I went out onto the landing and, after finding the right key, locked the door.

The courtyard was deserted although the flowing water in a fountain sparkled in the sunshine. I entered the mansion and found the back hallway empty. The activity seemed to be in the kitchen and dining room where I spotted Jeff and Eric. I scuttled past them, not wanting to talk, needing time alone. *My own space.* Grabbing my coat off the rack, I flung it on and went outside.

The street where I'd parked last night was crowded with cars. It was a busy thoroughfare, and after a few minutes, I was able to pull out of my spot, take a sharp right, and drive into the driveway alongside the house. I drove to a low brick wall that made up part of the courtyard, pressed the garage door opener, and swung my vehicle into the empty space inside the garage. There were two cars inside, a lovely red Acura TL and a practical Honda CRV. I guessed they both belonged to Jeff, or maybe one was Melissa's. I didn't know.

Collecting my large suitcase from the trunk, I closed up the garage, walked into the carriage house, and back up to my apartment.

My apartment. It still didn't feel right, but at least I was more comfortable away from the big house. That was a place I didn't belong. Some sixth sense told me so. I was an interloper, probably because of my drunken farm-boy father. Because of him I was not good enough for the Chadwick family. Melissa's own father had thought so, hadn't he?

But that didn't destroy my pleasure in unpacking and settling in. I hung up my few pieces of clothing in the huge walk-in closet, wondering how anyone could ever fill it up. Then I emptied the shoulder bag of all my facial soaps and cosmetics, arranging them neatly in a drawer near the sink. I lined up my vitamin supplements in a row in the medicine cabinet. Mom always called me a hypochondriac for taking so much expensive stuff, but I wanted to be healthy and thought all that "stuff" helped.

My final task was to prop Victoria in the middle of the bed. She looked much prettier against the pink pillow sham instead of that overelaborate bedspread from last night.

Finally finished, I stored the luggage in the walk-in closet. Then I opened the shutters and sat down at the desk, letting the sunlight flood the desktop. Plugging in the power cord to my laptop and connecting the cord to it, I powered it on. Using the Wi-Fi to check my email and Facebook, I found nothing interesting. I'd dropped out of my old life and nobody had noticed.

Oh, well, it was the present that interested me. That and the past of a woman I did not know. So I fiddled with the keys Jeff had given me and found one that opened the desk drawers. Inside the top drawer, I found a framed photograph of Melissa and a man who must have been her husband. Jeff was right. I did look like my real mother, so much so that it was scary. We had the same straight blond hair, and she had a certain sideways grin that reminded me of mine. It was eerie seeing her picture, seeing the woman who had given me life and loved me enough to give me up.

Why did she feel guilty? She'd done the right thing when she let me be adopted. Didn't she understand that?

On the other hand, I knew guilt. I knew the unexplained tightness in my chest and frequent upset stomachs. I knew the nightmares—vivid flashes of light and storm winds accompanied by an overwhelming anxiety. Mentally I understood I had no reason to feel guilty about being adopted, about the circumstances of my birth. The divorce of my parents and my mom's subsequent depression also weren't my fault. I could do nothing to cure her cancer and had supported her throughout her treatment, caring for her to the detriment of my own career goals.

Get on with your life, friends had lectured me. But I hadn't done that. Including a sense of responsibility, holding me back had been this nagging guilt. It stemmed, I suspected, from the unspoken message that I was the only reason for my mother's happiness. I couldn't abandon her, even if I wanted to, not until Mr. Carmichael's visit and our unexpected windfall, that is.

Propping a cheek on my fist and resting an elbow on the desk, I stared off at nothing. I remained that way for a long while going over my life, reflecting on my mistakes and lack of accomplishments. Let's face it. I had been sort of existing. Marking time with a life that was going nowhere.

Once again, I resolved to make something of myself. After the holidays, I'd register at the University of Louisville. I could go full-time now. I could get my degree faster. Until then, I must satisfy myself about my birth mother and about my heritage. Maybe then the strange guilt I felt would go away.

With a course of action decided, I dug again into the desk

drawers. Directly beneath the framed photograph was an album with more pictures. I didn't know those people, but the child looked like Melissa. I set the album aside and decided to look at it later. Underneath it was a manila, clasp envelope, probably nine-by-twelve, with my name written on it in black ink.

Elizabeth Abbot, it read in bold, flourishing strokes. Was this my mother's handwriting? I reached out and touched my name, as if that simple act would bring her closer and make her real.

My shoulders tightened with tension. I bit my lower lip. Not ready to open the envelope, I set it aside for the moment.

There was nothing significant in the rest of the desk drawers. Oh, a few pens and pencils and blank pads of yellow paper, but nothing like business files or personal memorabilia. It was like my mother had wiped the desk clean of herself. Did she do it when she got sick? Did she have that much time? Was she hiding something from me? Or in denial herself?

I couldn't guess. Not knowing her, I had no clue to why her desk, which should have been the most personal thing in her room, was devoid of anything that could give me a hint about her personality, her life. I was forced to turn to the envelope. Opening it scared me. But I had no choice.

Slowly, I lifted each edge of the clasp and pulled out the ruled, yellow paper containing the same black cursive writing as the envelope. There were five sheets, fully covered, and numbered consecutively. The first page was dated 18 September.

My Darling Beth, it began.

I cringed inwardly. My mom had never called me "darling" in my whole life. And here was this woman I didn't know addressing me intimately like that. It was weird beyond belief.

I read quickly. She explained about her diagnosis and that she knew her time was near. She told me about her guilty feelings because she'd abandoned me. She'd not been strong enough to stand up to her father, and by the time she'd matured and married, she'd lost track of me. The other lawyer had died. Hers didn't know where I'd gone. She let it rest, getting on with her life, until her husband Mac died. Then she started to look for me again.

Mr. Carmichael had told me these things, but it was different reading about them in my mother's own handwriting. It creeped me out, but I couldn't feel sorry for her. Not like I felt sorry for my mom, Sue. She hadn't been born with a silver spoon in her mouth, and she'd had a hard life. She didn't deserve the jerk she'd married and the way he treated her.

I picked up the third sheet of paper and leaned back in the chair away from the sunlight.

Jeff helped me find you, it read. *He has such gifts, but refuses to use them. He carries his own burden too that I hope he will one day exorcise. I feel it has nothing to do with 9/11.*

Now that was strange. I'd sensed something odd about Jeff—a connection thing, an attraction that I was too frightened to pursue. I hadn't been in this house, this place, long enough to understand the implications of what I'd gotten myself into. By agreeing to accept the inheritance from my birth mother, I'd hoped to help my mom. Was I getting into something more? Something dangerous? For my psyche if nothing else? After all, my history with men was a lousy one.

I read more. Melissa explained that she was overjoyed when she learned my name and whereabouts and that she followed me from afar until she got sick. Then she wanted to meet me. Make up for lost time. But time was something she didn't have, so she arranged for me to receive the money, the house, everything. In her mind, I was the rightful heiress, after all.

Jeff will help you, my dearest, Beth. Trust him. I've trusted him, and he's never let me down. I want you to know how much you are loved by me. Even though we never met, even though you were taken from my arms after the moment of birth, you have always been in my heart. Now and forever. Your birth mother, Melissa Chadwick Williams

There were tears in my eyes and a huge lump in my throat. For some odd reason, I felt the warmth of my mother's love engulf me. It sprang out from these pages into my heart. I swallowed hard and wiped away the tears. Now more than anything, I wished I'd met her. I wished there'd been enough time.

CHAPTER SIX

Fighting to suppress my sadness, I folded the letter, put it back into the envelope and locked it away. For several minutes, I scoured the rest of the apartment, looking for anything personal of my mother's. Just like the desk, there was nothing to be found. Didn't she want me to know her? Was the letter all I'd ever have of hers?

I sat down on the sofa and leafed through the photo album. Melissa's lifetime, in a nutshell, from childhood to marriage, was contained in the pages. It was almost as if she'd designed the book just to give me a glimpse of her life. Not enough to know her. Only enough to whet my curiosity.

Jeff knew her. Melissa said to trust him. Maybe he'd tell me about her if I asked. She also said he had a gift he didn't use, and I wondered what she meant. The thought of approaching him with questions made me nervous. He was so enigmatic. And my attraction towards him was perplexing, to say the least.

My stomach growled as I considered what to do next, making my choice obvious. I was hungry. I needed to eat. And there was nothing in the bare kitchen cabinets except for a few condiments and a bowl of sugar.

I took a few moments to clean up, brush my hair and teeth, things a woman would do if primping for a date. I grimaced at the thought of going on a date, but cleaned up anyway. Then I let myself out the apartment door, locked it, and pocketed the key.

The sunshine had faded into a gray afternoon. Crossing the courtyard quickly, I entered the hallway through the back door, and walked to the kitchen. It was a hum of activity. A catering staff, complete with a male chef in a white coat and toque, was preparing for the special banquet tonight.

Trying not to get in the way, I found a loaf of white bread and a jar of peanut butter and made a sandwich. I confiscated a can of Coke from the refrigerator. With my stash of goodies, I slipped out of the kitchen and into the library.

Sandwich in one hand and drink in the other, I wandered down one side of the room and then another, looking at paintings of dead ancestors and scenic shots of Old Louisville in the nineteenth century. The library smelled of musty books and leather. I faintly detected the scent of tobacco smoke and imagined the whiskered gentleman in one of the pictures sitting by the fireplace and smoking his pipe.

I loved the long walls of books. The floor to ceiling bookshelves were crammed full of old volumes. I was afraid to touch them, so simply surveyed them, soaking up their richness and grandeur. The library was cool and gloomy. It was quiet away from the hustle and bustle of the kitchen. It my one of my favorite places, next to my own apartment. I thought it wonderful and serene.

And then I spotted the oil portrait of a little girl. It hung over the mantle. I stared up at the child—blond curls, white frilly dress from another century, and a sweet innocent smile. I connected with her eyes, and she seemed to smile down at me as if she still lived and breathed.

Shuddering, suddenly cold, I knew this was my ghost come to

life. This was the little child who ran laughing through the bedrooms upstairs. I sat down hard on an antique loveseat and stared. It was if the child was speaking to me, pleading with her blue eyes and sweet, timid smile.

I had the strangest feeling I knew her, and *that* creeped me out. This house was unsettling—the antiques and the paintings, as if stuck in a century long past. I'm sure that was the attraction for guests to the bed and breakfast. Here, they got a taste of the past. A long-gone era of wealth and privilege. But I didn't belong to it, or this house, even though it was supposedly mine. I just felt out of place, and a sickness cramped the pit of my stomach.

Washing down the last of the sandwich with a drink of Coke, I set the empty can on an end table. The little girl's picture continued to draw me. Sitting back and resting my head on the love seat, I continued to stare at her. The room's ambiance settled around me, its mood and character, its quality of old affluence. I let it envelop me, hoping to soak up something from it, so that I would feel more at home.

With the little girl smiling down at me, I shut my eyes and soon drifted off to sleep.

Awaken by the sound of laughter, I sat up, confused, gathering my bearings. The room was dark. I remembered where I was. *The library.* Had I heard another ghost? But the laughter was real enough, and so were the tinkle of glassware and the clink of china. The dinner party must be in full swing. I heard the muffled voices mixing with laughter. I sensed the hustle and bustle of servants, coming to and fro from the kitchen to wait on the diners.

Somehow the noise was comforting, as if the dinner party was the most natural thing to happen in this house. And I guess it was. How many dinner parties had the Chadwicks hosted? How many of the city elite had passed through the doors of the house and dined in the very room that a modern-day businessman had reserved for the evening? It's as it was and as it should be, I thought.

The bed and breakfast needed to do more of these happy events. Of course, I didn't know how many dinner parties were hosted here, because I knew nothing about its operation. But if we didn't have many parties, then we should have more. And as owner, I'd make sure of it.

Listen to me. Making plans for something I knew nothing about.

My determination failed me. Who was I to make plans for this house? Just a poor girl from Bowling Green. Nothing special, no matter my mother.

Glumly, I scooted back on the loveseat and propped my right leg up on the cushions. Angled away from the painting that was shrouded in shadows, I had a better view of the light shining through the library door. I didn't want to chance leaving while the party was going on. I didn't want to run into anyone, so I sat in the dark library like a coward, listening and dreaming and wondering.

I don't know how long I stayed there. I heard the guests toasting the holiday and each other. The table was cleared, and dessert and coffee brought out. Someone gave a short speech. I heard the drone of his voice, but not his words. Then they stood to leave, gathering their coats, saying goodbyes.

The serving staff cleaned up. From my experience as a waitress, I imagined the routine. The dishes were washed and packed away. The back door opened and shut many times as they carted away their equipment. Finally, the noise and activity subsided. The back door closed. It was quiet. I rose and stretched. Leaving the library, I walked into the kitchen.

Instead of Corey at the kitchen sink, Jeff stood there with his back to me. I enjoyed being able to observe him without his notice. I stood at the threshold, taking in his tall presence and energy. Strange warmth suffused my heart.

"You might as well come in and join me for dinner," he said, without turning around.

Breathless, I fought the urge to run away. "Thank you. I don't want to intrude."

He faced me, dishtowel in hand, his dark eyebrows drawn over eyes that bore into mine. "You're not intruding. You own the mansion," he said, as if to remind me of the fact. "However, if you prefer to eat in your rooms, I can fix you a plate of leftovers."

That was the last thing I wanted. Isolation wasn't appealing. I'd already been by myself much too long today. I gave him a tentative smile. "I'd rather eat with you, if you don't mind."

"Of course, I don't mind, Beth."

He said my name again and a little thrill swept up the back of my neck. I dipped my head, letting a lock of hair shade my eyes. Then I gathered my courage and marched into the kitchen and hoisted myself onto a stool pulled up to the work island.

"How was the dinner party?" I found my voice weak when I spoke.

His back was to me as he pulled covered dishes from the refrigerator. "It went off very well. We've hosted these clients before, and they always have a good time."

"Is there anything I can do to help with our dinner?"

"No. I'm just going to microwave the leftovers the caterer left."

I nodded. He worked quickly and efficiently, scooping comfort food onto two plates.

"I should ask if there's anything you don't like," he said very business-like. "We have roast beef, mashed potatoes, and green beans."

"Sounds yummy to me." I ended with a little giggle, which sounded dumb.

Suddenly, I realized I probably couldn't eat a thing. Not with him there. Not with the nerves raw in my stomach. I shouldn't be this way. I'd never been good with guys, and this was the most handsome man I'd seen a long time.

"Let's take these into the back dining room," Jeff suggested after the final ding from the microwave. "The formal dining room has been cleaned."

"That's fine." I slid off the stool.

"What do you want to drink?"

"Coke. I saw some cans in the refrigerator." I stepped past him to open the refrigerator and found a can. I turned, looking up at him. Our gazes met and held. "Ah, I can carry my plate."

He handed it to me. It was warm from the microwave.

"Soft drinks aren't good for you," he said.

We walked into the dark dining room. Jeff flipped the switch and light flooded the space. I put my plate at the far end of the table and sat down. I popped the can top.

"You sound like my mother." I tried to make light of his comment.

"Just saying." He sat down by my side so that we were actually very near to each other.

I hated eating in front of people. It made me feel like a klutz. But Southern cooking wasn't called comfort food for nothing, so I ducked my head and dove into my meal, gobbling it up much too fast. When I realized Jeff was watching me eat, I felt the flush of embarrassment creep across my cheeks. I looked up. He'd only taken a few bites and my plate was practically clean.

"You must have been hungry."

He said it in a way that sounded critical. At least I took it that way. What right did he have to comment about my manners? What I ate and drank? I didn't tell him that, but it seemed as if he read my mind.

"I'm just concerned about you." He paused, cleared his throat, and forked a piece of roast beef. "Melissa wanted your welcome to be a happy one."

I watched him lift the fork to his mouth. He surveyed me as he ate the bite, as if daring me to reply.

What was I to say? How could I talk to this man who affected my senses in such a strange way? *Melissa.* She was the key to what bound us.

"I read Melissa's letter," I said, unable to say "Mother."

"Did you find what you were looking for?"

That was an odd question. I didn't know how to take it. Or how to answer it. What was I looking for? So I answered slowly, "I now understand how difficult it was for her, and how much guilt she felt."

He nodded. "I told her not to feel guilty. We all have free-will, and she exercised hers at the time out of love and respect for her father, not considering her later feelings about you."

"She did the right thing," I told him. "I had a good life."

He looked me directly in the eyes. "One you were probably meant to have."

I didn't understand his meaning. How could I have been meant to be born out of wedlock? With an adopted dad who was such a jerk? But I'd been loved by my mother. And now I knew Melissa had loved me and told him so.

"Melissa's love for you was the guiding force in her later life," Jeff replied, tilting back his head and relaxing in his chair.

"She said you helped her find me."

He sat forward then, dropping his gaze as if ashamed. "I located you, yes."

Was that it? Wasn't he going to tell me more? I didn't dare ask him about these gifts he was supposed to possess. Did he use them to find me?

"Well." I pushed back from the table. "You'll have to tell me more about Melissa some time. I looked at her photo album, but it was pretty sparse. She didn't leave me anything but the letter and the album."

"Melissa was a private woman."

"It appears so."

We sat silently a moment, inspecting each other, sizing each other up. It was awkward, and I didn't get it. This was the oddest damn thing that had ever happened to me. I was swimming in an emotional river and was unsure if I could make it to the other side.

"So, Jeff," I said deliberately calling him by name. "What's on the agenda for tomorrow?"

"Nothing really. The bed and breakfast is closed. Tomorrow night is Christmas Eve."

"And it's Sunday."

"We may have a white Christmas," he said. "The weathermen are all excited about it."

I stood and picked up my plate. "How romantic." I let the irony twist in my voice. I'd be stuck the rest of the holiday in a strange house with an equally strange man who was the age of my real mother.

Leaving the dining room, I went to the kitchen sink, washed my plate and utensils, and left them to dry on a dishtowel.

He was putting away the leftovers when I turned around. "We have enough for another meal," he said with his back to me.

I watched him doing simple, domestic chores remembering my mom and dad in our tiny kitchen doing the same thing. That was back when they were together, and we were a family.

"I think I'll find a church for services tomorrow morning," I informed him more to cover my own sudden sadness than to make conversation. "And then stock up my kitchen area, especially if it's going to snow."

"Sounds like a good idea."

He faced me. There was a look of yearning in his eyes. It was hard to explain, but I was drawn to him because of that look.

Shaking myself mentally, I fought that attraction. This was nuts. *I* was nuts. I couldn't have feelings for this secretive man who I knew nothing about.

"Will you have dinner with me tomorrow night?" he asked. "Here, in the big house. About six? It can get lonely on Christmas Eve without family."

Was he reading my mind? Or was he thinking about Melissa? He had no family either. "Sure. I'll be glad to," I said. Suddenly I felt a surge of confidence. "And maybe you can tell me a little about yourself, since my life appears to be an open book to you."

With that, I turned on my heel and strode from the kitchen. How's that for a dramatic exit? Give you something to think about, Jeff, I said to myself.

The short walk across the courtyard was cold, dark, and spooky. I hurried across and tramped up the steps to my apartment. Unlocking the door, I went inside and flipped on the lights. I found the controller and brought the flat screen TV to life. I wanted none of the dark shadows tonight. I wanted light and noise.

Retrieving my laptop from the desk, I brought it to the sofa and sat down in front of the TV. I didn't care what program was on. It was company. Booting up my laptop, I surfed until I found a church and a grocery store. On a wild whim, I searched for Louisville ghosts and discovered books written on the subject. I'd visit the Barnes & Noble tomorrow before it closed for the holiday. I could download the books to my Kindle app, but for some reason, I liked the idea of holding the books in my hands.

Nearing midnight, I shut everything down, turned off the lights, and went through the bedroom into the master bath. I got ready for bed, suddenly tired, my mind reviewing the day's events.

Only the bedside lamp illuminated the room when I crossed the floor to the king-size bed. Pretty and pink, I thought to myself, and reached down to toss back the comforter. That's when I noticed Victoria.

My heartbeat raced, nearly exploding in my chest. The hair on the back of my neck lifted in sudden fear. My doll was no longer in the center of the bed against the pillow where I'd left her. Victoria was face down in the middle of the bed—almost as if a child at play had dropped her.

CHAPTER SEVEN

Baxter Square Park, Louisville
Wednesday, March 26, 1890

"Come on, Lizzy, I'll race you to the fountain!"

My little charge darted away ahead of me. We had just entered the wrought iron gates of the park for our leisurely stroll, as Nurse had suggested, to release some of Miss Grace's pent-up energy. Often when Mr. and Mrs. Chadwick were away, as they were now traveling in Europe, Nurse, who was actually the governess, Miss Abigail Smith, would develop a migraine, leaving me with Grace's care.

I didn't mind. I was only sixteen, not much older than ten-year-old Grace. And I liked her. I liked the mischievous twinkle in her eyes and the ever-ready skip in her step. She'd go places, our Miss Grace would. She had spunk. I liked that too.

Following her down the wide walks that crisscrossed the park, I kept Grace in my sight. She wore a navy blue, sailor dress with a large, white, scalloped collar. Her skirt went to mid-calf, and she wore black high-button shoes. The day was warm enough that she didn't need a wrap. In fact, with the coming of spring, a tree canopy had already formed over our heads.

With the wind whipping my hair, I loved the freedom of the moment, because I rarely got time off. On occasions like this, I pretended what it would be like to be wealthy and pampered like Miss Grace. Only a chambermaid, I was lucky for a position in the big house. I made $1.25 a week, plus room and board. Ma hoped that I'd become a lady's maid eventually. I wasn't so sure, because I had a beau. Female servants were not allowed to marry and remain employed.

Miss Grace skittered to a halt at the fountain. She leaned over the stone base watching the splash of water. I came up behind her.

"Look! I have a penny!" She pulled the coin from a pocket. "Let's make a wish."

"I couldn't." Slowly shaking my head, I knew it wasn't right to take her money.

"If I say you can." Miss Grace put her little foot down. "You will."

"But I don't know what to wish for."

"Silly. We wish that your Bob comes calling again."

"If you want," I agreed, trying to hide my enthusiasm.

"I do, and you shall make the wish." She placed the copper penny into the palm of my hand and then closed my fingers around it. Her tiny hands cupped my chapped fist. "Now think on it, Lizzy. Deep in your heart. Wish for your Bob to come."

Shutting my eyes, I called out silently for Bob to whisk me away from a life of servitude and make me his wife. Opening my eyes, I glanced down at Grace's eager expression, her shining eyes.

"Ready?"

I nodded. She released my fist. "Now turn around and throw it over your back into the fountain."

I pivoted slowly, trying not to think of the horrendous waste of money. Hesitating, I squeezed the penny once and then tossed it over my shoulder. It splashed gently into the water. I turned quickly and watched it settle into the pool below. Watching it sink, Miss Grace had placed her hands and one knee on the wall and peered over the edge.

"There it is!" She pointed. Turning her head to gaze up at me, she said with the confidence of a child, "See now, Lizzy. He will come."

I gave her a tentative smile. "If you say so, Miss Grace. I believe you."

"Good." She stood up and took my hand. "You're the only one who believes me, Lizzy."

It was odd for a poor serving girl to be walking hand-and-hand with the daughter of one of Louisville's wealthiest businessmen. I knew she was lonely. Her older brother was at Harvard. Her parents traveled. In my mind, Nurse was insufficient company for an active, curious child who needed to be in school with other children.

We went along to the gazebo. It was empty. We stepped inside out of the sunshine and sat down.

Miss Grace looked down at her hands, being quiet for a minute. Finally, she said, "You know I see things."

"Yes." Of course, a child with a vivid imagination saw plenty things that us regular folk never had time to see.

"I see your Bob coming to visit." She turned her face upward. "You'll like that, won't you?"

Bob Torrance worked on a riverboat. He came from my part of town, and we'd known each other for many years. I nodded, yes.

"And I see all these trees toppled over and split in two." There was fear in Grace's voice when she spoke.

"Oh, surely not, Miss Grace," I said. "Such sturdy old trees."

"I know," she whispered. "It's sad."

"Let's not think of such sad things. The day is too pretty."

We went on to talk about the cardinals in the treetops and the squirrels scampering across the grass. Pampered squirrels they were. Living in the city, they probably would not find themselves at the end of a gun barrel and on someone's dinner table.

A little later, we toured the park. Only a city block, it was a fenced oasis. We skipped and sang and laughed as we walked around and around it. Finally, we approached the gate, and I saw Henry sitting there in the dogcart patiently waiting for us. Clyde, one of Mr. Chadwick's carriage horses, was hitched to the simple, four-wheeled vehicle.

"There's Henry. It's time to go," I said.

Miss Grace gave no resistance. She liked Henry. He was a big, man of color who had never married. Ma said he was married to his job and the Chadwick family. Ma said he was about forty. He seemed old to a girl like me. But his ready smile made him affable. I liked him too. Living above the stables, where the quarters were for the serving staff, I felt safe knowing he was below me. Always there. Always dependable.

"Here you go, Miss Grace." Henry lifted the child up to the second seat. "Miss Lizzy!"

When his hand clasped mine to steady me as I climbed aboard beside Grace, I felt a warm connection that flowed like maple syrup through me. I rejected the sensation and thanked him politely.

Then he turned Clyde around in the middle of the street, and we jogged down Jefferson Street to Third Avenue and home.

CHAPTER EIGHT

December 24, Present Day

Christmas Eve dawned gray and quiet. Enmeshed in the strange world of the night's dream, I stayed in bed, floating neither fully awake nor asleep. I wrapped my arms around my body, hugging myself, feeling alone.

Flashes of my dream came back to me slowly, but not completely. I thought I remembered a blond-headed child and a sunny, spring day. I thought I heard happy laughter. Other than that, the details slipped silently away as soon as I tried to recall them. I hated that about dreams. They seemed so real when you dreamed them, only to disappear in the morning's light.

After twenty minutes, I crawled out of bed and readied myself for the day. I'd made my plans and wasn't going to allow a half-remembered dream or speculation about who moved my doll change them.

Before leaving the apartment for the church service, I called my mom. She sounded glad to hear from me and wished me Merry Christmas. Her sister and family were treating her well. She missed me, for sure, and hoped everything was going okay. I lied, keeping my tone calm. Things were going well enough, so it wasn't a big lie. It's just that I was new to this kind of life and the people who populated it.

As we talked, I tried to suppress the ugly guilt that rose to my chest because I was not there with my mom. I told myself she wanted to go to her sister's house. My coming to Louisville would benefit us both. I wasn't responsible for her happiness, was I? Managing to tamp down my ever-ready feelings of responsibility, I wished her Merry Christmas, and we hung up saying we loved each other.

The large Methodist church in the eastern part of Louisville was welcoming, the choir superb, and the sermon uplifting. It was noon by the time I found the Barnes &Noble further east in a shopping center. The store wasn't too crowded, but there were some last minute shoppers. I wondered briefly about finding a gift for Jeff, but I hadn't known him long enough for that, I decided.

After browsing the aisles, I discovered a couple of books about ghost hunting in Louisville and bought them. Bookstores soothed me, the same way the library at the mansion did. I loved the shelves of books and watching the people who strolled the aisles looking for books. Not wanting to go home, needing the feel of companionship, I took my new books to the coffee shop and bought a scone and a mocha java. I found a place at an empty table where I could read and eat at the same time.

Old Louisville especially was full of ghosts, one book stated. According to experts, the solid foundations and the thick walls of the Victorian-era homes in Old Louisville accounted for the high level of paranormal activity. Each chapter of the books explored different homes and the accounts of people who had experienced supernatural events in them. The author gave no judgment about the truth of the events. He simply reported on sightings and the history of the places where the paranormal activity took place.

I found a chapter on the Chadwick house and read it with

interest. Much of its history, I already knew. However, I didn't know the supposed identity of the crying ghost. *Crying?* I'd only heard a laughing ghost.

The ghost was supposedly the daughter of Thomas Chadwick and his wife Isabel. Little Grace Chadwick had been only ten when she lost her life in the 1890 Louisville tornado. There was a fuzzy picture of the child, and it confirmed she was the girl in the portrait over the mantel in the library. Guests at the bed and breakfast had heard her crying upstairs. One even reported seeing a spectral child, murky like an old black-and-white movie, standing in the hallway. All reports talked of her crying and sadness.

The back of my neck prickled as I read about little Grace, and I wondered if my dream was important somehow to my under-standing. I wished I could recall what it had been about. Would it have provided more clues to go with the ones I just learned?

Around two o'clock, I left Barnes &Noble and found a grocery store before hitting the Interstate to go back downtown. I bought breakfast staples and peanut butter and bread.

I wasn't sure about the schedule at the bed and breakfast. Would Jeff let me to help with breakfasts for the guests? Or was I supposed to sit on my keister all day and look pretty? I reflected that life for the well-to-do women in the nineteen hundreds must have been really boring. All their entertaining and society watching would have made me crazy.

I drove home, parked my car, and went upstairs. Jeff had said six o'clock for dinner, so I had time to kill. I didn't want to go to the big house, because I felt more comfortable in Melissa's modern apartment, so I flipped through the second book, got bored, and turned on the TV. *White Christmas* was on, and I watched it again for the umpteenth time.

Later, before going to the big house, I cleaned up—brushed my teeth and put on fresh lipstick. I put on my black, wool trousers that I wore this morning and my soft, red cashmere sweater. It wasn't dressy, but it was the best I had with me.

An old-fashioned light that looked like a streetlamp lighted the pathway from the carriage house to the backdoor. It hadn't been turned on the night before. I wondered if Jeff had turned it on for me tonight. The backdoor was unlocked and the hallway also lit.

The door to the kitchen was shut, but the one to the main reception hall stood open. I went through it and glanced at the bright and cheery Christmas tree, enjoying its scent.

Jeff welcomed me at the door to the drawing room with its red drapes, striped sofa, and painting of seventeenth-century women hanging over the mantle. He wore comfortable gray corduroys, a lighter gray turtleneck, and the red cotton cardigan sweater with a zipper down the front. He was sort of like a shabby professor. Yet, I found him endearing in a weird way. And when he smiled at me, I returned the smile, my stomach suddenly feeling empty.

I was hungry, of course. Nothing more. I didn't care about the way his blue eyes perused me or the way his hand was warm when he touched my elbow and escorted me into the room. That was such an old-fashioned gesture I couldn't help wondering if this place wore off on people eventually. Did we all feel like we'd stepped back into the nineteenth century when we lived here?

He seated me in front of the fire on the striped sofa. "Would you care for a drink before dinner? Or a glass of wine?"

"Wine, I suppose." I wasn't much of a drinker. We'd never done that in my family, because my mom's dad had been an alcoholic. Yet, I wanted to be polite and not look naïve.

"Do you prefer red or white?" Jeff asked. I watched his halting steps take him to the bar cart near the door to the dining room. The top was crammed with bottles. Glasses were stored underneath.

"If you prefer dry, white wines, dry and oaky, Chardonnay is good with turkey. I also have a Sauvignon Blanc that's also good."

"Turkey?" I thought I'd smelled something delicious.

He turned and grinned. "I felt like cooking. Leftovers didn't cut it for Christmas Eve."

His smile tied my tongue. Seriously, I didn't trust my feelings with Jeff and was on guard immediately. I cleared my throat and dropped my gaze. I'd always heard red wine was better for you, so I told him I preferred red.

"Pinot Noir is a perfect fit for the holiday dinner," he said. "It's more robust than white wine."

"Then that's what I want." I chanced a glance at him. "I'm feeling rather robust tonight."

What in the hell did I mean by that? I had no clue. It had just slipped out of my mouth. Was I flirting with Jeff? Did he think so? I saw him grin and look away. He must think me really lame.

He brought me a pretty, stemmed wine glass. When I accepted it, our fingertips touched, sending shock waves rushing through me. Dropping my gaze, I refused to look at him and felt my cheeks flush.

Jeff sat in a chair angled toward the fire and sipped his wine, staring at the cozy blaze. I watched him a moment and then brought the glass up to my lips. The bowl of the glass was so wide that I couldn't comfortably fit my fingers around it, but was reluctant to hold it by the stem. I took a sip. Not familiar with wine, feeling awkward and naïve, I thought it had a kick to it, but not an unpleasant one.

"Pinot Noir was once described as sex in a glass," Jeff commented peering into his glass. "It's been called the most romantic of wines."

Was he just making conversation? Surely, he meant nothing more. We'd just met. These twinges and stirrings I experienced had nothing to do with anything romantic. Surely, Jeff had no ulterior motives tonight.

Why did I even think such a thing?

I wiggled uncomfortably on the stiff sofa and downed a rather large gulp of wine. Too large, I found out, but managed to get all the liquid down without choking.

Jeff glanced up and gave me a half-smile. "How was your day?"

The way he said it made me even more ill at ease. He was a mature, good-looking man, and I felt like a kid in his presence.

"Very nice," I replied, lifting my chin for courage. "I found a friendly church and spent some time at Barnes &Noble. Did you know this house is supposed to have the ghost of a child upstairs? I found it in a book about ghosts in Old Louisville."

I didn't say I'd seen the apparition. I spoke as if I was just making conversation too. It was Jeff's turn to squirm in his chair. He looked uncomfortable, but recovered with a nod of his head.

"We're quite famous for our little ghost," he said. "I believe some people book rooms simply hoping to see her."

I sipped my wine, gazing into the red liquid, thinking about how far I wanted to take this conversation. Should I admit I'd seen her?

Glancing up, I said, "The book says the ghost cries. I'm wondering if it is the little girl whose portrait is in the library."

"Yes, it's Grace."

The way he said her named seemed so intimate, as if he'd known her. But if he'd been working here for a long time, I'm sure the portraits hanging on the walls became like old friends.

"How long have you been here, Jeff?"

"I came in 2002." He glanced at me, his gaze soft and warm. "I ended up here after 9/11. Melissa needed help to run the business. She needed even more help after her husband died."

Was that when he found me for Melissa? Soon after he arrived. I longed to ask him about his mysterious gift, but found my tongue really tied. "Melissa was lucky to have you," I said in a guarded way.

He shrugged. "She always told me that." Then he stood

quickly. "Bring your glass to the table. I'm hungry. I don't know about you."

Standing, I followed him to the table where he set down his glass and headed toward the kitchen. There was no extra help tonight. "Do you need me to do anything?" I asked.

"No," he called. "Have a seat."

Dinner that night was turkey with all the trimmings, a delicious cranberry orange relish, mashed potatoes, tossed salad, and homemade yeast rolls that reminded me of my grandmother's. Well, Sue's mother, that is.

I told Jeff how good the food tasted and asked him where he learned to cook. He said he'd picked it up after coming to work for Melissa, but he'd always been interested in it.

"What did you do before?" I asked at one point.

"Finance," he replied and looked away.

I got the feeling he didn't want to talk about himself, and because of that, I didn't know what else to say. Yet, by the time the lack of conversation turned really awkward, dinner was over. Jeff suggested we go back into the drawing room and told me he'd clean up later. He asked if I wanted coffee.

While I waited for him, I stared at the fireplace. The fire was burning low, but continued to add an aura of coziness to the formality of the nineteenth century room. I grew sad missing my mom and all that was familiar. Fearing the change that had been thrust upon me, I wondered about my future. My thoughts eventually turned to the past, the past of this house. How could Mr. and Mrs. Chadwick have survived the loss of their only daughter?

"They didn't very well," Jeff said coming into the room with a silver coffee service.

He placed the silver tray on the small, vintage coffee table in front of me.

"Excuse me?" Had I asked the question out loud? I didn't think so.

"You asked how the Chadwick's survived losing little Grace," he told me, as he poured steaming coffee from the silver decanter into a china cup and then handed the cup and saucer to me. "Cream?"

I nodded yes, weighing the fact that he seemed to have read my mind.

"They were devastated," Jeff commented and offered me a cream pitcher. "Over one hundred people died that tragic day of the tornado. They didn't make it home for the burial, leaving that to the servants." Jeff sat down and balanced his coffee cup and saucer in his hands as he gazed at me. "Mrs. Chadwick died in Paris the next year, people said of a broken heart."

His heartrending words settled over me, and I almost felt like weeping. I knew how my mom acted when anything bad happened to me, like the time I broke my leg. I could imagine how she'd feel if I'd been killed tragically like the little Chadwick child.

"So sad." I sipped my coffee and then glanced up. "It's no wonder she haunts the house."

Jeff wore a pained expression. I saw the wretchedness in his eyes before he turned them away from me. It was really strange that we were sitting here on Christmas Eve talking about an event long past. This was the strangest Christmas Eve I'd ever experienced.

Jeff set down his cup and saucer and stood. "I don't mean to be gloomy," he said trying to act brighter by forcing a smile. "I have a Christmas gift for you."

"You do?" *Oh, my gosh!* I should have trusted my first instinct at the bookstore. "I don't have anything for you."

"It's not from me," he said quickly, pulling a small, black box from behind a candlestick on the mantle. "It's from your mother."

The way he said the word "mother" startled me. I shuddered inwardly and gazed up at him, trying to hide my feelings of uncertainty.

"Melissa wanted you to have it for Christmas." He handed me the box.

Still seated, I accepted the velvet jewelry box, and glancing up, our eyes met. He stepped back, giving me space. My heart thumped as I tentatively opened the top. Inside on the black cushion was a gold locket.

Our gazes met again. "For me? Really?"

"It's 14k yellow gold," he told me, explaining what was inside. "Isabel Chadwick received it for Christmas in 1890. Hand engraving is nearly a lost art form. That's one reason it's so special. Years later, Melissa received it on her sixteenth birthday. She used to keep a photograph of her husband in it."

I was enchanted, but, yes, uneasy. The antique hand-engraved locket was something valuable. Removing it from the box, I held it in the palm of my hand. Carefully, I opened the top that was covered in minute floral engraving. The inside was empty except for the original glass.

My mouth was dry. I was close to tears. Something about Melissa's gesture touched me to the core.

"I wish I could tell her thank you," I said in a scratchy voice.

"She knows."

I wondered about his remark. About his calm certainty. Swallowing my sudden emotion, I stood and offered Jeff the necklace. "Will you put it on for me?"

He stepped nearer. "Turn around."

Lifting the gold chain over my head, Jeff draped the necklace around my neck. His fingers fumbled with the clasp, his breath warm against the top of my head. His presence behind me was intense. I felt the specter of his tall body against my back, as if his energy transferred to me and warmed me.

"Merry Christmas, Beth," he said in a voice soft and spiritual. "May this day be the start of a wonderful new life for you."

I clutched the locket now hanging securely around my neck. If

I turned, I'd be in his arms. The depth of this realization reverberated through my suddenly hot body.

"Thank you," I answered breathlessly.

And then I pivoted. He was standing behind me as I suspected, but his hands were at his sides. His gaze, though, caressed me. It felt almost a lover's embrace. I couldn't explain it, or my unexpected desire. My lips parted. What did I expect? Or want? A kiss? From a man I'd just met?

His eyes flashed and then he turned his back on me. "I'd better clean up."

"Don't you need my help?" I wanted to stay. I wanted to be with him and explore these strange glances and sizzling emotions.

"No, another time. Get some rest."

I wanted to tell him I didn't need to rest. I needed companionship. Friendship. Not isolation. I wasn't used to being alone with my thoughts.

But I chickened out. "Okay. Good night, then."

"Good night." He lifted the silver tray, his back remaining toward me.

I walked toward the main reception hall and halted at the arched doorway. "Merry Christmas, Jeff," I said loud enough for him to hear me across the room.

He stopped a moment and then without acknowledging me, continued toward the dining room with his halting step.

My fist remained closed around the locket. Releasing it, I wiped my damp palm on my pant leg. I headed, heart heavy, through the reception hall. At the Christmas tree, I paused to enjoy the sparkling colored lights.

That's when I heard a giggle. I whipped around to catch sight of a white skirt skipping up the staircase and disappearing on the landing above. The skirt was gossamer, translucent, unreal.

Wow!

On Christmas Eve Grace Chadwick had paid me another visit.

CHAPTER NINE

December 25, Present Day

The snow started during the night. When I awoke around eight in the morning, I discovered the snow was falling heavily outside. Everything in my line of vision—the courtyard below my window —was white. The only movement came from the continuing spray of water from the fountain and the falling flakes of snow.

Why is it that the world seems different with snow on the ground? At peace. Slower. More accepting of nature and God's creation. The world outside my window was beautiful, and I wrapped myself in delight as I watched the huge flakes drifting through the air.

After a while, I thought about returning to bed, but wasn't tired. Instead, I put on a bathrobe and went into the living room and turned on the TV for company. Nothing interesting was on the regular channels. It was Monday and Christmas Day. Normal programming was interrupted, so I turned on HGTV and let a contractor describe how he remodeled a basement to make a rental property for the homeowners.

While I was eating my breakfast of cereal, my mom called. She sounded lonely. I was too, because this was the first time in my life I'd not spent Christmas with her. We talked a bit and then said good-bye.

Was this change in my life going to work out? Granted, I'd only been here a few days, and the days were mixed up because of the holiday, but I seriously doubted my ability to fit into this big home and its routine. I needed a life of my own, and right now Chadwick Bed and Breakfast felt like a throwback to another era, one that I didn't comprehend or have any desire to understand.

The only thing that interested me at all about my whole situation was little Grace. Melissa had used the ghost's presence to market her establishment. The Chadwick Bed and Breakfast was on the city's ghost tour and described in a book. Jeff had said guests came simply to catch a glimpse of the apparition.

One question intrigued me. Why had her spirit remained in the house? Did the tragedy of her death have something to do with it?

Wasn't there a way to send spirits away? Back to wherever they were supposed to be? I was clueless about the concept, but I'd seen the movie *Ghost* with my mom on TV. It was her favorite. And I remembered the Patrick Swayze character being sent into the light at the end of the movie. It seemed that's where Grace's ghost belonged. In the light. Not racing through the dark and drafty upstairs halls of the Chadwick Bed and Breakfast. Either crying or laughing, it didn't matter. She didn't belong here.

After cleaning up the dishes, I stood at the window and again watched the snow fall for a while. It was coming down steadily. I wondered how many inches we'd get. It didn't matter. I had nowhere to go anyway.

Tired and bored from lack of activity, I eventually took a shower just to make myself feel better. While in the shower, I reviewed my encounters with Jeff. I knew only a little more about him now than I'd known a couple days ago. He said he'd been at the bed and breakfast over ten years since 9/11. He'd been in finance before that. But nothing more. Nothing about where he came from or how he got his limp. Had he been in the military? Was it a war wound? I found speculation intriguing. Just as I found the man intriguing.

Hold up! I told myself while drying off. Remember your track record with men, I said to myself. Unable to explain my attraction to Jeff, I was doubly leery of it. Been there, done that too many times. Being burned by bad choices had been my regular operating procedure until I'd wised up and quit dating at all. Abstinence had been my solution to my problem of picking wrong guys.

I dressed in jeans and a flannel shirt. Hesitating only a moment, I pulled the hand-engraved locket from my small jewelry box where I had put it for safekeeping and draped it around my neck. The gold was cold for a few seconds until my body warmed it. For some reason, the locket felt good there. As if it belonged. Then I went into the living room.

What I needed was a good book to read to take my mind away. A good romance with a happy ending, that's what I needed. I wanted certainty, and a romance novel was a sure thing, because no matter what trials and tribulations the characters went through, the reader knew the hero and heroine would end up together at the end.

I needed such assurances now when my own life was in flux. Maybe Melissa's money was a godsend, but that remained to be seen. Melissa's death and her will had thrown me into a strange world alone—a world that frightened me if I was honest with myself.

I was flipping through the ghost books, the TV blaring, when a knock on the door scared the hell out of me. I jumped sky high, or so it seemed. After my heart settled and the knock sounded again, I went to the apartment door and slowly opened it.

Jeff stood there in the shadows wearing his trademark turtle-neck and sweater.

"Hi," he said a little sheepishly. "I was wondering if you'd like to join me in my apartment for lunch?" Before I could say anything he rushed on, "I brought the turkey over last night and the other leftovers. I was afraid it would snow, and thought I'd rather have it with me instead of opening up the house today."

As I stared at him, he shifted his stance from one leg to the other. His black hair was a little long, curling at the nape of his neck. *Dang, he was cute.* I was always a sucker for curly, black hair. And, OMG, his blue eyes bore into mine from under long eyelashes, as if they could see right through me into my very soul. *To hell with the age difference!*

"What do you say?" He cleared his throat. "I don't bite, you know."

Was he as aware of our apparent attraction as I was? Or did he even feel the pull? God only knew, because I didn't. And I'd already decided today to be cautious. Not wanting a repeat of my past performances with men, I didn't want to make the same mistakes.

But here I was seriously considering accepting Jeff's invitation. After all, it was snowing outside, and where else did I have to go? I was poor company for myself. It was Christmas Day, for crying out loud.

"Sure," I found myself saying. "I'll be glad to share leftovers with you. Let me get a sweater."

A few seconds later, I shut my apartment door, locked it, and pocketed my key. As I followed his shuffling gait down the steps, he commented over his shoulder, "I'm glad to see you so cautious."

"What?" I'd just chided myself for *not* being cautious, and here he was praising me for that.

"Locking your door."

"Oh?"

"This is not the safest part of town, so you can't be too careful, even on a snowy day."

Can't be too careful and here I was willingly heading into the lion's den. But Jeff Halstead didn't seem like a lion to me, more like a cuddly pussycat. Mysterious—sure—and standoffish like many cats, but one I'd dearly love to get my hands on and stroke.

A sudden flood of desire shocked me. My whole body flushed with it. I was hot and shivery at the same time. *What in the hell is going on?* I'd never had such an intense reaction to a guy before. Now I really had to watch myself, be cautious like Jeff expected, or else I was afraid I would want to jump his bones and make a real fool of myself.

Fortunately, we didn't have far to go. The roof covered the stairs to my apartment. Snow was piling up just a few steps away in the courtyard. Jeff's apartment entrance was under my staircase, so we didn't have to dodge snowflakes.

Yet, I paused on the wooden porch to take a deep breath of the clean, cold air and bridle my emotions. Jeff paused too, and I felt him behind me.

"It's beautiful," I said a bit breathlessly.

"And quiet. The streets haven't been plowed, yet, so traffic is scarce because of it."

"And because it's Christmas Day too, I guess."

"Yes. Everything stops at Christmas."

Except my libido, I perversely said to myself. Then I drank the cold air into my lungs, savoring it. Maybe cold would douse the heat I felt within.

"We'll catch cold," Jeff said. "Let's go inside."

I had to shake myself mentally, because the way he said it almost sounded like a lover's invitation. *Stop it! He's nearly old enough to be your father.*

Then sucking it up, I turned and smiled. "Yes, it is getting cold."

We marched to his apartment door like good little soldiers. Suddenly, I knew he'd felt our connection. I knew he had, but I didn't know how I knew. There was just something there between us. And I realized I needed to keep this something at a distance.

Jeff's living room had a "man cave" feel to it, thanks to a deep, plump sectional wrapping around walls painted gunmetal gray. A square parquet coffee table, topped with a geometric mosaic of wood pieces, filled the space between the sections. The sectional faced an elaborate media center with a flat screen TV and stereo equipment. A framed sepia-toned Taj Mahal reproduction photo hung on one wall.

Like my apartment, the kitchen was situated in the far corner of the rectangular living space and separated from the living room by a bar with wooden stools pushed underneath. Jeff headed directly there while I stood looking around. I liked the feel of his space, its comfortable and manly feel. My hands clenched briefly, and then I released them. Why did this space turn me on? Because it belonged to Jeff, of course. Because I had the hots for him.

Damn! Stop it!

Aware of my own heartbeat, I perched on a wooden stool and was very glad for the countertop separating us. Then I watched his swift efficiency as he pulled out the sliced turkey in a plastic bowl and the other leftovers.

"Sandwich or warmed over leftovers?" He turned and made firm eye contact.

"Sandwich," I said, "if you have mayonnaise and sweet pickles. They're the best with a turkey sandwich."

He grinned and turned back around. "I must have read your mind. I bought both yesterday at the store."

I sat back and crossed my arms. That was a weird thing to say. Just last night I'd wondered if he read my mind.

"What do you want to drink?"

"Coke, if you've got it."

"The real Coke or another kind of soda? I know around Kentucky the word 'coke' takes the place of soda or pop."

"Real Coke, if you please. I'm addicted to it, I'm afraid. And I don't like Pepsi."

Jeff pulled a Coke can from the refrigerator and a pitcher of dark liquid that he told me was tea. "I'm addicted to that," he revealed. "I keep a cold pitcher in the refrigerator all the time."

"Sweet tea?" Like mom used to make, I thought.

"Yes, it's the best, isn't it?"

I nodded, feeling a bit more at ease. Slowly, I'd get to know him, wouldn't I? The thought cheered me, and as he handed me a plate with the turkey sandwich and sweet pickles on the side, I allowed myself to smile at him.

He smiled back, slowly letting it build, until he ducked his head and turned to pick up his plate and glass of tea.

"Do you want to eat in front of the TV? We can watch a movie."

"Sounds great."

I hopped down and headed to the sofa, setting down my plate and Coke can on the coffee table. He sat beside me and picked up the controller.

"Have you seen *Argo*? It came out last year and won an Oscar. I recently rented it on Netflix."

"What's it about?" Biting into my sandwich, I chewed it slowly. I didn't tell him I wasn't much of a moviegoer.

"A CIA operative who led the rescue of six U.S. diplomats from Tehran during the 1979 Iran hostage crisis. I was only a kid at the time, so I'm fuzzy on the details."

"Well, given that I wasn't even born...." I let my voice drop off and then glanced at him with a grin.

"Okay, quit it. Don't rub it in."

Jeff punched a few buttons and the movie started. We finished our sandwiches and then sat back on the cozy sofa. I slipped off my shoes and put my sock feet on the coffee table. Then I thought better of it and dropped them quickly.

"Go ahead." I heard the grin in his voice. "Melissa used to do that too."

I returned my feet to the coffee table. The action barreled ahead in front of us on the screen, but I only watched it with part of my mind. I wondered about his comment. Did he mean that I was like my birth mother? How many times had he and Melissa sat like this watching a movie and conversing? Suddenly, I was jealous of the woman I didn't even know.

When the movie finished, Jeff stood up and removed the plates as the credits rolled. He came back and sat down beside me. "Want to watch another one?"

"How about something lighter?" He flicked through the choices, and I spotted *Ghost* on the list. "Hey, how about *Ghost*? It has its funny moments."

I caught his look toward me. I turned my head to meet his gaze and shrugged my shoulders. "In honor of our house ghost," I said.

He looked uncomfortable a moment. "Sure," he finally replied. "How do you know about *Ghost*?"

"It was my mom's favorite."

"*Dirty Dancing* was my favorite Patrick Swayze movie," Jeff reflected. "Nobody puts Baby in a corner," he said in a gruff voice after the famous line from the movie.

I giggled. The impersonation was so unlike him or my perception of him, that is.

"We can watch it next," I suggested. "My mom liked it too."

I must tell you, the opening scene with Patrick Swayze and Demi Moore making love over a potter's wheel and clay pot to the tune of *Unchained Melody* was downright erotic. I hadn't thought much about it when I'd seen the movie with my mother, but it was all I could do not to look at Jeff during that scene. As it was, I wiggled uncomfortably on the sofa, hypersensitive to the heat surging through my body.

He stood at the end of the scene and left the room without a word. I stared after him, but quickly drew my gaze back to the TV when I saw him return. There was a U of L stadium blanket in his hands. He draped it over me.

"Melissa was cold natured," was his only explanation as he returned to his seat beside me on the sofa.

Did he think I squirmed because of the cold? *Boy was he wrong.* Nevertheless, I *did* appreciate his thoughtfulness about the blanket and snuggled under it.

At one point in the movie, Whoopi Goldberg's character Oda Mae explained, "He's stuck, that's what it is. He's in between worlds. You know it happens sometimes that the spirit gets yanked out so fast that the essence still feels it has work to do here."

Was that what happened to Grace Chadwick? Was she stuck because she had something else to do?

Once again the movie ended the same as I remembered. Patrick Swayze's character Sam defeated the bad guy and evil spirits, and then he turned toward the light. "It's amazing, Molly," he said to his wife. "The love inside, you take it with you."

Chills coursed up and down my arms. How profound. God is love, and surely Sam was going toward God. I bit my lower lip and hugged the blanket closer.

We were quiet when the movie ended. I couldn't move. "Do you think it's really like that?" My voice was hushed.

"No, I don't think mediums really see ghosts the way Whoopi Goldberg's character saw them."

Was Jeff intentionally misunderstanding me? "No, I mean ghosts being stuck between worlds and being able to take love with you when you die?"

"Yes, it is possible to be stuck between this life and the afterlife," he said with quiet reverence. "God's love is the basis for all existence. That and the vibrant energy of the universe. It is possible to take love with us, because it's never far from who we are as spiritual beings."

My breath faltered. I leaned toward Jeff, wanting to touch him, but not wanting to disturb the ethereal look on his face. There was a glow about him. I couldn't look away.

"I've seen her." My voice was full of wonder. "I've seen the ghost."

His gaze turned towards mine. "You've seen Grace, the child?"

"Yes." I reached out and touched Jeff's sleeve, but he didn't seem aware of my action. "You're right. She didn't look like a person. Just a wisp of white. An impression. A movement. And I heard laughter."

He moved closer to me. "Beth, you heard her laugh? She wasn't crying?"

"No. She even giggled."

His face turned gray. He placed his hand against his chest, fingers splayed out, as if he was making a pledge.

I was suddenly alarmed. "Is something wrong, Jeff? Have I done something wrong?"

He leaned back, shaking his head as if he wanted to create space between us. "No, no, nothing wrong." Was he gathering his thoughts? "We're quite famous for a crying ghost," he said with an ironic smile. "I hope this doesn't hurt business."

I raised my eyebrows at his insensitive comment and sat back. The moment was lost. Jeff turned and picked up the controller.

"How about another movie?"

I watched another one with him. We saw *Dirty Dancing*, and I found myself wishing for Baby's spunk. Then we ate more leftovers, and it was time for me to go home. I wanted to anyway. I wanted to figure out what had happened between us today, and that kind of reflection took distance and solitude.

Before I left, he asked for my cell phone number, in case he ever had to contact me. I watched him punch my numbers it into his iPhone. Then he gave me his cell number and the number for the house, just in case, he said. I thanked him for his thoughtfulness and for lunch and dinner. We parted as polite strangers.

Jeff followed me outside and stood at the foot of the staircase as I walked up the steps. When I got to my door, I unlocked it and glanced at him. He was looking up at me from below. I hesitated, and we favored each other with our gazes. Then I nodded my head once and fled inside, escaping the cold night air and the strange bond vibrating between us.

I went straight to the bathroom and got ready for bed. It wasn't very late, but for some reason I was exhausted. When I went to turn down my bed, I noticed Victoria propped against the pillow where she belonged.

But this morning when I'd made the bed, I'd left her in the chair near the window.

CHAPTER TEN

December 26, Present Day

I didn't dream. At least I didn't remember any dreams. I awoke late in the morning to find the snow had not melted during a cold night. Gazing out my bedroom window at the courtyard below, I saw someone had already cleared a path from the carriage house to the big house. Scraping noises sounded nearby as if someone was shoveling the driveway.

After cleaning up and gobbling down a bowl of cereal, I threw on my overcoat and a pair of old shoes and left the confines of my apartment. I couldn't stay cooped up today, not with the snow and cold air beckoning. Outside, I saw the city had plowed the streets. The scraping noise I'd heard earlier came from Eric. The unfortunate fellow was shoveling the length of the driveway.

"Good morning," I called to him.

He stopped, rested his gloved hands on the handle of his shovel, and grinned at me. "Good morning, yourself."

"Did you have a nice holiday?" Why was I making pleasant small talk with the guy when I'd had such a negative reaction to him earlier? But he was technically my employee. I could be gracious, couldn't I?

He shrugged. "It was okay. Nothing special."

I thought about my day spent with Jeff. Had it been special? Yes, I suppose it had been. I still felt the glow from it reverberating deep within.

Immediately, I responded to that warm feeling by disavowing it to myself. There was nothing between Jeff and me, nothing but a silly sexual attraction on my part, the kind that had never gotten me anywhere nor done me any good.

"I enjoyed seeing the snow," I said to Eric. "But I guess you don't care much for shoveling it."

I crossed the path he'd already cleared and stood at the edge of the driveway. He gave me a calculating grin, surveying me from head to foot. An uncomfortable sensation passed through me. Yet, I held my ground, determined not to let him bother me.

"It's a job," he answered rather casually. "Pays the bills and gives me several perks."

I didn't like the look he gave me. Was he insinuating I was a perk? "Well, I'm glad," I said as if I hadn't thought anything about his remark. "I'd best get inside out of the cold."

I turned to leave and saw a shadow disappear from the downstairs window of the carriage house. Was Jeff spying on us? Or me? I glared at the window, but avoided glancing at it for more than a second, turning instead to go into the big house. There I found Corey bustling around the kitchen. She was a ray of sunshine, and I was immediately cheered.

"Good morning," I said as I removed my coat.

"Good morning, Miss Abbott." Corey stopped and smiled.

"For heaven's sakes, call me Beth. I certainly don't feel old enough or wise enough for you to call me Miss Abbott."

"Beth, then." She ducked her head and turned to the stove. "Have you had breakfast?"

"Yes, but I could use a cup of coffee."

She poured a mug of hot coffee and brought me the half-and-half in a carton right from the refrigerator.

"Just like home," I told her, and we shared smiles.

After that, she scooted herself up onto a stool at the butcher-block island, and we sat a few moments together quietly sipping coffee. It was a companionable silence. I was grateful for it and her.

"What are you going to do today, Corey?" I finally asked.

"We have guests arriving tonight, so I'll make sure the rooms are ready. I have silverware to polish and laundry to do."

"Is there anything I can help you with?"

"That's not a good idea, is it?"

Miffed, I frowned. Jeff wasn't the boss of me. Yet, I wasn't used to making waves. I didn't want a repeat of my earlier scolding.

"I wish there was something I could do around here," I said recognizing the whine in my voice.

"Mrs. Williams cataloged old photographs. You might enjoy looking at those," she suggested.

"Really? Where are they?"

"In the library. One of the drawers in the desk, I believe."

"She left me an album of pictures, mostly herself and her husband."

Corey glanced over the rim of her cup. "These are older ones. Maybe you'll find pictures of our child ghost among them."

"You mean Grace Chadwick," I said with a shallow sigh.

Cocking her head, Corey shrugged a shoulder. "She was a Chadwick. She could be there."

Excitement fluttered in my belly. I slipped off the stool. "Thanks, Corey. That's a good idea. Have a good day, okay?"

After pouring more coffee and stirring in more half-and-half, I carried my mug into the library with is musty book smell. For some reason, my eyes prickled with tears as I surveyed Grace's portrait over the mantle. The child's innocence radiated from her face. The artist had captured that well. I was drawn to her eyes, but this time recognized sadness in them. Or maybe it was the loneliness I knew she felt.

How did I know that? Maybe because I felt so alone and had seen the same sad look in the mirror this morning.

On my past visits to the library, I had not paid attention to the lovely, wooden pedestal desk in the far corner by the window. I suspected it was an antique. The top had a black leather inset with gold tooling around it, which was still in good shape. The chair behind the desk also appeared to be antique. It swiveled and rolled, and looked as if it could hold the stoutest Victorian gentleman.

Sitting down, I touched the desktop with reverence. Could my grandfather and his father have sat in this chair? I don't know why I had become sentimental. I hadn't known these people, and they had made a point of disowning me. Yet, I had a dulled awareness that this home had been important to my life, if only because this was where my real mother had been born.

The drawers were unlocked. I opened the bottom one to discover a set of leather-bound albums. Lifting them out one at a time, I noticed each one was inscribed with a date. I picked out one labeled *1890s* and opened it.

The first picture was of this house probably taken soon after it was built. The sidewalk in front looked new and without cracks from overgrown tree roots. In fact, the only trees appeared newly planted, and the front of the house was bare of any landscape plantings.

Another fascinating picture must have been taken in the spring because the trees in the background appeared to be in bloom. A carriage that looked like a stagecoach and four matching horses had been pulled up in front of the house. No one rode inside the carriage, but sat on seats on top. The driver was a man in a formal suit with a top hat. His passengers were four, fancy-dressed women with their long skirts and big hats and three gentlemen riding on what appeared to be jump seats in the back. A black man also neatly dressed and wearing a top hat stood in front of the horses.

I flipped through each album finding pictures of Thomas and Isabel Chadwick, their son Thomas Jr. There were pictures of Thomas Jr. as an adult and his wife and children. The family history albums progressed through the twentieth century until I spotted childhood pictures of Melissa with her parents, my grandparents.

But there were no pictures of little Grace.

What had happened to her? How had she died? Was the memory of her death so painful that her family had destroyed all her pictures? I longed to know.

Lifting my hand to Isabel's locket hanging around my neck, I wrapped my fingers around it. Had Grace's picture once been encased in its elegant hand-engraved frame?

A few minutes later, I heard Jeff arrive recognizing the deep timbre of his voice. He talked to Corey in the kitchen, but I couldn't hear what he said. My body smoldered with warmth. What was wrong with me?

I put away the photo albums and strolled into the kitchen. Watching from a distance, I gauged Jeff's mood. He looked distracted, but focused on the guests who would arrive this afternoon. He also looked awfully good. I don't know why just seeing him brightened my spirits.

He turned, and his gaze darted toward me. Instead of saying hello, he turned back to Corey giving her last minute instructions. Then he headed into the dining room away from where I stood. I scurried after him like a toddler chasing an older child.

"Jeff, wait."

He stopped and glanced back. Turning toward me, he surveyed me with an arrogant glare.

Opening my mouth to criticize his lack of greeting, I stopped short. I forced a smile. "Thanks again for feeding me yesterday. I had a good time watching old movies."

"I'm glad." He was curt, his posture rigid.

"I was looking at Melissa's old albums. There's a really neat picture of a horse-drawn carriage in front of the house."

"I've seen it. The driver is Thomas Chadwick." His gaze shifted away. "Listen, Beth, I am really busy now."

"Oh, sure." I said in a controlled tone. Of course he was busy. He had a business to run, and I was just an inconvenient interloper. "I'll talk to you later."

Backing up a step as he headed into the front part of the house, I lifted my chin. It wasn't the first time I'd been rebuffed by a man. Yet, Jeff's rudeness hurt. But why should I care so much? I told myself I didn't even know him. I'd spent Christmas Day with him, but he'd only been kind because of the snow and me being new to town. It wasn't like we were dating.

Afraid I'd do something stupid like cry, I rushed out the side door of the dining room away from Corey who remained in the kitchen. I lifted my coat from the rack in the back hall, slung it on, and headed out the door. I really needed something to do that didn't tie me to this house and its occupants, living or dead. I couldn't wait until the university opened again, and I could enroll in classes.

Eric was outside finishing with his work. "Hey!" he yelled at me.

I couldn't rush past him, or I would be as rude as Jeff Halstead. I paused and gave him a half-hearted grin.

"Want to go sledding?"

His question came out of the blue, completely unexpected. "Sledding?" I asked in a stunned tone.

"A bunch of us are going to Dog Hill this afternoon. It will probably be crowded, but it is a lot of fun."

"Sledding?" I repeated myself. It sounded fun, but going with Eric? I wasn't sure about that.

He must have understood my hesitation. "Corey said she'd join us after she finished up here."

I glanced at the big house. If Corey was going along, then it should be safe enough to join Eric.

"When are you leaving?"

"As soon as you're ready." He gave me a shrewd grin. "Unless you need to ask Jeff's permission."

I squared my shoulders. I didn't need to ask permission of anyone. Jeff wasn't the boss of me. "Sure. It sounds fun. Can you wait until I grab my gloves and hat?"

He winked. "I have all the time in the world."

Going sledding with Eric was a daring thing to do, and I felt adventurous because of it. Not my usual risk-adverse self. I needed distraction and fun, I told myself. I was sick and tired of this big house and this whole damn awkward situation.

Persuading myself this was a good thing to do, I ran up the steps. Inside my apartment, I had the presence of mind to grab a few dollars and my cell phone along with my gloves and a knit hat. I made sure I locked the door before I left to trot back downstairs where Eric waited for me near his old Ford truck.

Dog Hill in Louisville's Cherokee Park never lost that name even after the city built a fenced dog area in another part of the park. Eric told me its history during our ride through streets now blackened with snowy slush. Baringer Hill, as it's officially called, isn't for the faint of heart on a snowy day. I stood at the top of it, looking down its long and steep incline wondering if I would chicken out.

"You'll be in for a wild ride," Eric said. "Are you up to it?"

If I'd wanted adventure, I was going to get it. The hill was crowded with teenagers and adults. A few children were sprinkled here and there, but this was definitely not a beginner's hill.

"How about you going first and showing me how," I replied with a grin. "That is if you're not afraid."

"Listen, lady, this doesn't scare me." Eric said it with a cocky wink. "I'll show you how it's done."

With that, he got a running start and flung himself belly first onto his elongated plastic sled. It wasn't a round saucer like so many people were using, but one with a pointed nose that probably was designed for speed. I watched, laughing, as he hurled down the hill until he was practically out of sight, a mere speck in the distance. What must have been ten minutes later, he finally climbed to the top of the hill returning to my side out of breath, his cheeks flaming red from the cold.

Eric handed me the rope tied to the nose of the sled. "Your turn, ma'am."

Determined not to let my courage fail me, I took the sled, walked down the hill a little ways to where snow remained packed, dropped the plastic vehicle to the ground, and sat down cross-legged. I paddled with my gloved hands, digging my fingers into the snow, which had basically turned to ice.

The ride started slowly, but picked up speed until I was soon flying down the bumpy slope. Cold wind stung my face. My blood rushed with exhilaration as I held on for dear life. All too soon, I was at the bottom, swerving to avoid a tree, and then toppled sideways as I skidded to a stop. After picking myself up and brushing myself off, I trekked up the hill.

The sled was surprisingly lightweight and easy to pull during my hike. Panting hard, I wondered about my sanity. It wasn't often that I saw my life flash by me like I'd seen during that ride. Exciting, yes. Smart, no.

I finally reached the hilltop where Eric awaited laughing at me. "You look like you've seen a ghost. Was it that scary?"

That was a strange thing to say. I'd seen a ghost, but he didn't need to know it. "You can't tell me it didn't frighten you."

"Hell, yes! But part of the fun is being scared shitless."

I wondered about his choice of entertainment.

"C'mon. Don't be a party pooper. Ride with me on this trip."

I didn't want to go again, but neither did I want to be a party pooper. Next thing I knew, Eric would call me chicken. I couldn't have that.

"Okay, one more trip. Then I need to go home."

"Ah, we've just gotten started," he said. "Our lips aren't blue yet from the cold."

Thank, God. But I held my tongue. Eric dropped the sled and motioned me to climb on board. "Sit in the front."

I scooted near the pointed nose and grabbed one of the two sets of handles. Eric placed his hands on my back and gave me a shove. The sled started to move almost like a two-man bobsled team in the Olympics. Before we had picked up too much speed, Eric jumped in behind me. His long legs circled my hips so that they stuck out in front of me. Instead of gripping the second set of handles, he grabbed me around my shoulders. His hands clutched my breasts under the layers of clothing.

Eric's body was athletic and solid. I hadn't realized how big he was until he enveloped me in a super bear hug that seemed to squeeze the life out of me. We zipped down the hillside together, wind stinging my cheeks, my hands clutching the handles for dear life. But all I could feel was his hard-on pressed against the small of my back.

I knew what he wanted. I knew what he was ultimately after. And I didn't like it one bit. In fact, terror wracked my body making me tense. We veered left to avoid a tree, careened off a rocky ledge and flew through the air—bodies and sled—landing in a snow bank.

Suddenly, he was on top of me, kissing me. I couldn't stop him. I couldn't push him away. Panic seized my lungs and throat. I couldn't cry out. Tears of frustration seeped out of my eyes as I twisted my head side-to-side trying to get his lips off mine.

"You're so beautiful," he murmured, finally relenting and raising up.

His eyes burned with desire. I recognized the fanatical aspect of the glow within his gaze. He frightened me. The fear lay deep within my heart, turning it as cold and frozen as the snow I lay in. There was no way I could have stopped him if he hadn't stopped on his own.

This has happened to me before.

At that thought, a strange calm stole over me. I lay quietly and looked up at him. "I'm getting wet and cold," I said to him in a voice that didn't sound like my own.

Something snapped Eric out of his obsessive behavior. He rose to his feet, grasped my hand, and pulled me up. "Let's go."

He didn't apologize or explain. He simply held my hand, seized the rope to the sled with his other hand, and led me up the hill.

God, I'd made a big mistake coming here with Eric. You'd think I'd learn.

Jeff stood at the summit when we arrived. His countenance was dark with a piercing scowl.

"Mr. Halstead!" Eric's face flushed with humiliation.

Ignoring Eric, Jeff directed his ire at me. "Miss Abbott, you're needed at home."

I was never so glad to see anyone in my life. Warm gratitude flooded over me. I didn't know how he'd found us or why he'd shown up, but to me it was like he'd come to my rescue just in the nick of time. Almost like a knight in shining armor.

"We were just having a good time," Eric blubbered.

Had he seen Eric kissing me?

"Let's go." Jeff put his hand on my back and propelled me down the slushy road.

Once, I glanced back to see Eric looking after us. Something told me his stare didn't bode well for me, but with Jeff as my champion, I didn't care.

We reached his silver gray SUV. "Get in."

I clambered into the passenger side, hardly caring that his words were clipped and angry. I was just so thankful that he'd saved me, because I really felt that he had.

Strapping in with the seat belt, I glanced sideways as Jeff climbed into the driver's seat. "How did you know where I was?"

"Your mother told me."

Confused, I cocked my head. "Sue?"

"No, Melissa."

A chill deep and icy raced through my body. Without thinking, I lifted my hand to my collar seeking to connect with Melissa's locket.

It was gone.

CHAPTER ELEVEN

We didn't talk on the way home. I didn't know what to say, being so shocked that I'd lost the antique locket. Unable to bring myself to tell Jeff, I sat like a zombie and looked out the window. Nausea gripped me as I reviewed the past few hours. What had possessed me to go with Eric? Had I been out of my mind?

As we drove up the long driveway beside the big house, Jeff cleared his throat. I glanced at him, but he was looking straight ahead. We pulled into the garage, and he turned off the ignition. Now I was in for it.

"I've given Corey time off for the holiday," was all he said. "I need your help for a few days. We have guests coming this evening."

The oppressive feeling in my chest lightened. I ventured a smile. "I'll be glad to help."

"Good. Clean up and meet me back inside the mansion."

Given orders that I was only too eager to fulfill, I jumped out of the car and sprinted up the steps to my apartment. Funny thing. I still had my keys and dollar bills. I hadn't lost those. Only the precious locket. Somehow I had to find the words to tell Jeff. I knew it wouldn't be easy.

The guests were a retired couple from Cincinnati who were in town to visit their grandchildren. The Martins found it too daunting to actually stay in their daughter's house. With four rowdy boys, the place was a zoo. They much preferred the quiet ambiance of The Chadwick Bed and Breakfast. Having stayed before, they knew what to expect and had even encountered the ghost.

As I led them up the grand staircase, the wife chatted quite openly about their experience with little Grace.

"Such a sad situation," Mrs. Martin said. "To be seeking your mother so many years after your death."

"Do you think that's why she's here?" I asked and unlocked the door to the Derby Room where I'd stayed earlier.

"Yes, why else would she be so sad and crying?" Mrs. Martin swept into the room ahead of me. I followed, and then Mr. Martin came in with the two suitcases. "She misses her mother. Don't all children?"

"I know how that is," I said, realizing I missed my mother Sue not the one I didn't know.

Seeing the room again where I'd spent my first night, I couldn't quite accept Mrs. Martin's assessment of the situation about the ghost. In my experience, Grace had been a happy ghost. I could almost hear her laughter as it sounded down the upstairs corridor.

"You're new," Mrs. Martin commented as she removed her coat. Her husband found his way to the bedroom. He disappeared inside to drop the luggage. I heard the television go on.

"Yes, ma'am," I replied, turning to speak to her directly. "I'm the new owner of the house."

"You are?" Mrs. Martin's voice lifted with curiosity.

I didn't want to get into it with her. She was probably a busybody, and I didn't welcome her kind of attention. I handed her the keys. "You are welcome to come and go. We lock the outside doors at seven o'clock. Breakfast starts at seven in the morning and continues until ten."

She accepted the keys. "We'll be closer to ten, dear. Jeff knows what to expect from us. Tell him we're in for the night. It's been a long day with the boys."

I nodded and turned to go. "We're glad to have you," I said and softly shut the door.

Back downstairs I found Jeff whipping up muffin batter for tomorrow's breakfast. His back was to me when I entered the kitchen. I noticed he favored his left leg, the one that must have been injured at some time. I wondered about it again. How it had happened? Would I ever gather up enough nerve to ask?

"They're settled for the night," I said.

He glanced around. "Thanks for taking them to their rooms."

"You needed my help," I replied. "I was glad to do it." He'd yet to chide me for my afternoon sledding escapade.

"I'll need you for breakfast tomorrow."

"Before seven?"

"No, seven should be good enough. The Martins are late risers."

"Do you want me to do anything else today?"

"Keep me company."

His request blew me away. My breathing stalled for a split second. Then it came out in a rush of astonishment. "Sure," I said.

"Are you hungry?"

"Sure." My voice faltered.

"How about pizza?"

"Sure."

I was a loquacious conversationalist, wasn't I? For some reason, Jeff's presence made me tongue-tied. I felt so young and inexperienced with him. Around him my heart beat quicker, and my body temperature rose.

I hadn't figured out what was wrong with me yet. I didn't want to think the "L" word—how ridiculous would that be—so I put it out of my mind.

I climbed onto a stool and rested my elbows on the countertop.

"What do you like on your pizza?" His voice was so deep and sexy. I loved the way his black hair curled at the nape of his neck.

"Everything, but anchovies," I told him, hoping I didn't sound like a schoolgirl with a crush.

"I'm calling Impellizzeri's on Main Street," Jeff said. "Their pizzas are famous in Louisville." He pulled his cell from a pocket and punched in the number for the pizzeria. As he ordered, he glanced at me. Our gazes connected, and a chill skimmed down my arms. I turned my head a moment. When I looked back, he was putting the batter away and cleaning up his mess.

"When do you take down the tree," I asked because there was nothing more to say. I didn't dare delve into the problem of the missing locket. That thought shot daggers into my heart. I was afraid of his reaction.

"Not until New Year's Day," he replied as he worked. "We have a New Year's Eve party here."

That was news to me, but I'd seen how the dining room had been rented out before Christmas so it made sense.

When the pizza deliveryman came to the front door, Jeff went to answer it. I scooted off my stool and watched his hitching steps down the hall. He paid for the pizza and locked the door. Carrying the box, he returned slowly, his gaze never leaving mine as he walked down the long hall toward me.

"Let's eat in my apartment," he said, making his off-the-cuff invitation sound like a request to go to bed with him. "Maybe we'll watch another movie."

My heart must have pitched into my stomach, because I felt

sick. Sick with anticipation, excitement, dread. A sane woman with my track record would say no. But I'd been silly enough to go sledding with Eric. I knew I'd be just as silly about Jeff and go with him. I trusted him more, for one thing.

And then there was that strange connection between us that I was terrified to explore.

CHAPTER TWELEVE

The pizza was wonderful. Instead of Coke, Jeff poured me a glass of red wine. I don't know what it was and felt too unsophisticated to ask, but it was delicious. I'm afraid I drank too much too fast and got light-headed.

I also lost my inhibitions. Or some of them that is. Still reeling from my near miss with Eric this afternoon, I couldn't curb my tongue as it delighted in the heady taste of wine.

"I was wondering," I said in a low voice as I stared into my wine glass, "how you got your limp." We were sitting together on the leather sectional much as we'd sat yesterday. The lights were dim, romantic. The television was not yet turned on. "I know it's none of my business. I'm just wondering if your leg hurts."

When I glanced up, he was surveying me with a warm look. "I've only told Melissa," he said. He hesitated. "I guess I can tell her daughter."

I shook my head. "No, not if you don't want to."

Jeff favored me with a weak smile. "I find that in the most desperate way I do want to tell you."

I reached over and set down the wine glass on the coffee table.

I'd had enough of that stuff. It had already worked to loosen my tongue. But I was gratified that Jeff wanted to talk to me.

"I got it on 9/11," he said. "September 11, 2001, the day the United States was attacked by terrorists."

I swallowed hard and stared at him, horrified. "Were you there that day?"

"Yes, on the fifty-ninth floor of the South Tower, Tower Two. When the first tower was struck at 8:46, I was in my office at Morgan Stanley."

I gaped at him with a new light of understanding. No wonder he'd been in Louisville since 9/11. He'd not wanted to return to New York City after that terrible day.

"The moment the plane struck the other tower I heard this ghastly boom and felt the building shake. I grabbed my desk to keep my balance. Then I ran to the nearest office window, one that faced west looking toward New Jersey. All I saw were chunks of burning metal, papers, desks, and bodies falling from the other building."

Horrorstruck, I watched Jeff's face contort as if he was seeing it all again. Of course, he was. How could anyone forget such a terrible thing?

"It was if the world was on fire," he said in a low whisper. "I stood at the window and watched, unable to move. And then I heard someone say to me in a clear, high-pitched voice, 'Get out, Jeff.'"

He took my hand. His was cold, but damp.

"I didn't know what was happening, but I knew I was in danger," he said. "Maybe a helicopter or small plane had hit the tower next to ours, or maybe something had struck up higher in my tower. I didn't know. So I rallied a few of the employees already in the office that day, and shepherded them into the emergency stairwell."

I was mesmerized by his story and couldn't unglue my gaze from his face.

"That's when I heard the same voice say, 'Get out and focus'."

Jeff and his group made it to the fifty-second floor before others joined them coming out of lower floors. The descent was orderly, but fast. When they reached the forty-second floor, the public address system announced that a plane had struck Tower One. At the thirty-eighth floor, another announcement came on telling people to stay where they were because it was unsafe to go outside where debris was falling.

"I heard another voice tell me to keep going and not to stop," Jeff said. "My fear was so strong by this point that I doubt I would have stopped anyway, but this sharp inner directive was too convincing for me not to listen to it."

Jeff described how he left the emergency stairwell a few seconds before the second plane crashed into the upper floors of Tower Two. At that time oxygen was sucked out of the building, and as he explained it, his lungs. He was in the first floor lobby by this time where the elevators there serviced floors three through fort-three. The turnstile was locked, so he was unable to run for the revolving doors that led out of the lobby and into the mall under the plaza level. Overhead he heard explosions inside the building. He knew he would die. And then the voice ordered him into a small space next to the turnstile and a support beam.

Jeff huddled in that tiny cubby hole-like space when the entire building shuddered and groaned and a horrific explosion rushed down the inside of the elevator shaft, an airplane fireball that exploded into the lobby and circled the walls, licking toward the small area where he'd taken cover. Then a giant section of burning wreckage fell into the street that ran parallel along the south side of the tower and smashed through the lobby behind where he hid.

"That's when I whispered what Christ cried out on the cross," Jeff told me. "Father, into your hands I commit my spirit!"

But he didn't die. He wasn't killed that day.

Water from the sprinkler system began to fall. Black smoke smelling of jet fuel poured through the lobby.

He left his sanctuary and picked his way over glass and debris reaching the revolving doors to the underground mall. There he crawled through a smashed window where the broken shards of glass slashed his leg. Joined by other survivors in the mall, he made his way to the Borders Bookstore at the end of it. There he finally emerged outside onto Church Street where he saw the extent of the destruction.

"I walked back to my apartment on 74th street. I didn't realize until later the extent of my injury, but it was a small price to pay. So many had paid with their lives that day."

His voice was hushed, full of pain. I ached for him, for what he'd lived through. For what he had seen. For what he'd survived when others had not.

"Oh, Jeff," I uttered softly. "I'm so sorry this happened to you."

And then he pulled me into his arms, wrapped them around me, holding me as close as two people could be. His kisses rained down on my face, covering it with his passion. And then his lips found mine. I kissed him, and he returned my kiss as if we were long-lost lovers who had been separated and were now reunited.

My heart was full of him, bursting with relief. I was so thankful he'd been spared. That he'd found his way to Louisville, and somehow I'd found my way to him.

"Oh, Jeff," I said against his lips. "You are so lucky."

He pulled back, gazing at me, brushing the hair away from my eyes, cupping my face in his hands. "Don't you see, Beth," he said. "Luck had nothing to do with it."

I turned a quizzical gaze at his.

"Those voices. They were my spirit protectors, my guardian angels."

Still I didn't understand.

"After that day, I knew I could hear them." His voice was urgent as if begging me to understand. "Don't you see, Beth, I'm clairaudient. I can channel spirit."

CHAPTER THIRTEEN

I didn't understand what I'd heard. "You mean you're like Oda Mae Brown?"

He gave me a sheepish smile that was oh, so cute. "Not quite. Like I said, I only hear spirit. I can't see them. This is not an exact science. I am just a translator."

"But I saw the ghost upstairs. I heard her laugh too."

"You're more psychic than you know," he said quietly.

I sat back. "But you must have heard her."

"I've only heard her crying."

I frowned, confused. "That's what I don't get. She's a very happy, little ghost. Why does everyone think she's crying?"

"Because she *is* crying when we hear her."

The ghost, forgetting for a moment that I'd been in Jeff's arms, and he'd kissed me, obsessed me. "Mrs. Martin, the new guest, thinks the ghost is looking for her mother."

"She's looking for someone, but I don't know whom," Jeff revealed.

"You've talked to her?" My voice rose disbelieving.

Jeff ran his fingers through his hair, rumpling the longish

strands even more. "I've tried to help her go home—to heaven—but couldn't convince her."

"You couldn't convince her?" I echoed, thinking about Patrick Swayze walking toward the light.

"No. She's stubborn." Jeff shook his head. "And she's not ready. She has something more to do on the earth plain."

I considered his answer, and then I considered him. Jeff had just revealed his profound secret to me, the one he'd revealed only to Melissa. He'd taken part in one of the worse disasters in American history and had survived because he'd heard and obeyed spiritual voices.

And then I remembered Melissa's letter to me.

Jeff helped me find you, it read. *He has such gifts, but refuses to use them. He carries his own burden too that I hope he will one day exorcise. I feel it has nothing to do with 9/11.*

I now understood what she'd meant about 9/11. That part made sense. But the rest of it didn't.

Reaching my hand out, I touched his sleeve. Our connection was deep and profound. I didn't have to be psychic to know it.

"In her letter, Melissa said you helped find me. How did you do that?"

"When I was learning how to hone my skills, I practiced automatic writing. That's when a person connects to spirit and writes whatever comes to mind on paper. I knew Melissa was desperate to find you. I wanted to help. When I tried automatic writing, I wrote your name. Several times I tried it, and every time I wrote 'Beth Abbott.' From then I researched the Internet. You weren't hard to find once I trusted in what I was being told."

"Can you hear Melissa now? Now that she's dead?"

"Yes. She told me you were in danger."

Disbelief rolled through me. I bowed my head, unable to look him in the eye. How could I admit the liberty Eric took with me?

After all, I'd gone with him against my better judgment. It must have been my fault by leading him on.

I glanced up. "My mother told you where to find me today?"

"Yes." His voice was firm, but quiet.

I was in awe of him. Would he know that I'd lost Melissa's locket? Did psychics know those kinds of things without being told?

"This is all very weird," I said, crossing my arms over my chest. "Tell me something Melissa has to say to me."

"A test?" His eyes squinted, lit with a mischievous twinkle.

"Yes, a test." I sat up straighter, challenging him.

Cocking his head to the side, as if listening, Jeff stared over my head a moment. "Yes, thank you," he said, talking to someone I could not see.

Turning his gaze back to me, Jeff smiled. "Melissa says you shouldn't drink so much Coca Cola."

"What?" I exhaled quickly. "You're kidding me?"

"No, she was very serious. She said the sugar in the drink is bad for you." He favored me with a knowing look.

"That sounds like something you'd say," I baited him. "Why would a ghost say that to me?"

"Melissa is not a ghost," Jeff told me very firmly. "Her spirit, her soul, is alive outside the earth plain. She's gone 'home.' Sometimes her energy communicates to me, like this afternoon when she knew you were in trouble."

Looking away, I wouldn't acknowledge the truth of that. "So, she's not like the child ghost?"

"No. She's crossed over. The child, Grace, is stuck here on earth for whatever reason."

I clung to that knowledge, for I didn't like the idea of my birth mother spying on me from beyond the grave. It bothered me. Much as the knowledge that Jeff could talk to her seemed weird.

Was it only a matter of time before Melissa snitched on me and told Jeff I'd lost her antique locket?

Only moments earlier I'd been kissing Jeff, and he'd been kissing me. Now the bond between us scared me even more. I didn't trust men very much and was unsure about trusting Jeff. He must have read my mind, because he started to backpedal.

"About that kiss earlier..." he said, glancing away as if afraid to meet my eyes.

"It shouldn't have happen," I finished for him.

His gaze flew up, his eyes softening. "You understand."

His voice was too eager. I wasn't sure what I knew, but I sensed he wanted to erase those intimate kisses. I didn't need to be psychic to read a man's body language. So I shrugged, not saying anything.

Jeff went on. "Melissa entrusted you to me at her death. I'm sorry I took advantage of you."

I opened my mouth to say something, but stopped short. I drew a deep breath and held it. Then I said, "Look, you don't have to explain anything to me." I stood up. "My behavior was inappropriate. You're much too old for me anyway."

I read the insult on his face, but didn't care. My mind was whirling with my own insecurities and questions. I'd always felt out of place, not belonging to my adopted parents and now surely not belonging in the Chadwick Mansion. If the spirit of my birth mother couldn't help me, then I'd help myself.

I sensed the key lay with the child ghost. For some reason, her laughing spirit and mine connected as nothing else connected, not even this strange attraction to Jeff.

"Thanks for dinner," I said with a stiff formality. "I need to be getting to bed. We have guests to feed in the morning, remember?"

Jeff rose to his feet, towering over me. "Yes. I remember." He ushered me to the front door and opened it. "Good night, Beth."

The way he said my name tore my heart. "Good night, Jeff," I said, lingering on his name and hoping he didn't hear the way I'd caressed it with my voice.

CHAPTER FOURTEEN

Thursday, March 27, 1890
Third Avenue, the Chadwick Mansion

Just as Miss Grace told me, Bob Torrance came calling the next day. He was fresh off a riverboat that had brought him up the Mississippi and then the Ohio from New Orleans. He smelled of exotic perfume and his black hair was slicked back off his forehead and mustache trimmed. I could tell he'd cleaned up in one of the boarding houses on Main Street near the riverfront. And my heart thrummed a little, because I knew he'd gussied himself up for me.

He moseyed up to the back door. I'd seen him from the upstairs window, thanking God that the Chadwick's were gone and Nurse was resting in the sitting room with a cup of Irish tea. I rushed down the back stairs and met him at the door even before he knocked.

"You look mighty pretty, Lizzy, my girl," he said with his deep Southern accent. His parents had brought him to Louisville as a child from Alabama, but he'd never lost that bit of the South when he talked.

I felt a blush sweep up my cheeks. "Thank you, Bob."

It had started to rain. I couldn't invite him into the house. It wasn't proper, me being a servant. I surveyed the back yard and the stables beyond. I couldn't take him upstairs to my quarters either. That certainly would have been wrong.

"Let's go into the stables and talk," I suggested and offered him my hand.

He clasped it, and we ran across the cobblestones to the stables. The barn where the Chadwick's stabled their carriage and riding horses was as highfaluting as their mansion. Built with the same bricks as the house, the barn walkways were paved in cobblestones. The stalls were huge, bigger than rooms in most homes, and bedded with cedar shavings.

I always found something comfortable about being in the fancy barn, among the scents of manure and hay and the sounds of rustling horses. Today, with the rain outside, the windows were shut and it was dark inside. We stood just within the door, as if Bob was afraid to venture any farther into the barn.

It didn't matter to me. I was so happy to see him that I would have stood out in the rain with him—if my knees didn't go weak. My tongue felt tangled, and a rush of euphoria overtook me.

"I'm only here tonight," he told me and squeezed my hand possessively.

"Oh, no! I was hoping you'd be here longer."

"Not to be, sweet lady. We must make due with tonight."

My lower lip jutted forward, and I dropped my gaze. "I must take Miss Grace to her dancing lessons tonight."

He scowled, his black eyebrows drawing downward. "Isn't that the job of her governess?"

Glancing up at him, I pursed my lips and shrugged. "Nurse says she has a headache. She does this every time the Chadwick's are away from home."

"Why do you have to take the child?" Bob's voice rose with anger.

"It's my job." I touched his sleeve. "Just like yours takes you away from me."

His face softened. "We must make the best of it then, Lizzy dear."

"How?" I questioned him.

"Where are the dancing lessons?"

"The Falls City Hall."

"Great. It's near the riverfront. I'll meet you at the back door at seven."

"But I can't leave Miss Grace," I protested.

"You're not leaving her. She'll be inside taking her dancing lessons. You're just stepping out for a breath of fresh air."

When I continued to look doubtful, Bob cupped my face with his hands and planted a big kiss on my lips. I almost swooned.

"You must come, Lizzy," he said. "I have something for you."

That settled it then. He had my curiosity up and my hopes. Was he going to give me a ring? Was he going to ask me to marry him?

"I'll come," I said breathlessly.

"Good!" He gave me another sloppy, wet kiss, but I loved it. "Got to go. See you at seven. Don't chicken out on me. Promise?"

"I promise."

And then Bob was gone, slipping out of the barn and making a run for it. He'd be drenched by the time he reached a streetcar stop. I took it as a mark of how much he loved me. Just as I loved him.

I stood a moment silently watching the rain, my fingertips lightly touching my lips where I'd been kissed so magnificently.

"Has that scalawag done gone?"

I jumped out of my skin at the sound of old Henry's voice booming behind me. Whipping around, I was mortified that Bob and I had been caught together. But it was only Henry. What did he matter?

"Bob paid me a visit," I replied with a lift of my chin.

Henry came out of the shadows toward me. "That boy's no good, Miz Lizzy. You have no business being with him."

I took offense, standing up straight. "We love each other."

"Psha!" Henry came closer. "The no-account means you nothing but trouble. Mark my words."

"Well, I don't know what you have to do with it, Henry." I set my shoulders and glared at him. "It's no business of yours."

"May not be, but the Chadwick's employ me to watch after their own. And I figure you work for them, so you're my responsibility too."

"Well, I don't need your care," I said with a huff.

We surveyed each other—he with a warm concern flowing from his eyes, me with a glow of defiance. Henry was right. I knew it in my heart that I had no business stepping out with Bob. But no man had ever paid any attention to me in my whole life. I didn't want to end up like my mother with a passel of kids and no daddy to take care of them. Bob would marry me and turn my life around. Why couldn't Henry see that?

Breaking eye contact, I said, "I've got to get back inside."

With that I took off running through the rain to the mansion, all the time wondering if Henry had heard us talking as well as seen us kiss. Did Henry know I had promised to meet Bob tonight? And would he do anything to stop us?

CHAPTER FIFTEEN

December 27, Present Day

At six o'clock, the radio alarm clock switched on to the broadcast of a morning radio show. I peeped open one eye and stared out from under the covers toward the dark windows. The remnants of my dream hung over me like a pall. Fear gripped me, my chest painful with it. But worse than that was a shroud of shame that engulfed me for no reason.

For a second, I wanted to quit this charade of respectability and wealth and return to Bowling Green where I belonged.

But I didn't, of course. My mom was going to surrender her apartment at the end of the month. I had nowhere else to go, so I was stuck with the life Melissa had forced upon me.

I crawled out of bed and showered and dressed. Wanting to beat Jeff to the kitchen, I hurried through my tasks. I was in the kitchen making a pot of coffee when he walked through the door.

The kisses of yesterday were a barrier between us. They entered the room with him. I ducked my head.

So, this is where the shame came from, I thought. I shouldn't have kissed him. Melissa had entrusted him with my wellbeing and throwing myself on him was not the right thing to do.

But he had kissed me first, hadn't he?

I was confused and covered my confusion with busyness. I pulled out two mugs for our coffee and got half-and-half from the refrigerator.

"I can set the dining room table," I said, "but you'll need to tell me which dishes to use."

Jeff must have felt the tension simmering between us, because he got right to work too. "Use the ones in the dining room china cabinet," he instructed. "You'll find silverware and cloth napkins there too."

I glanced at him to see him surveying me with a warm look. Could he read my mind? Just how psychic was he? Unable to fathom his abilities or his thoughts, I turned my back on him and got to work.

It didn't take long to set the table for two. I was back in the kitchen soon, feeling like a fifth wheel, not knowing what to do or what was expected of me.

"We have time to eat breakfast before the Martins come down," Jeff said. "I don't expect them before nine."

"Okay." I was cautious. Did he regret telling me about his experiences? Was he sorry he kissed me? If he wasn't going to mention last night, neither was I.

"If you want orange juice, you can pour it. I'll take a glass too."

"Sure." Feeling better for some direction, I found juice glasses in the overhead cabinet and pulled a carton of O.J. from the refrigerator.

I set two places at the bar, and by the time that was done, Jeff was shoveling scrambled eggs and fried potatoes onto my plate. I sat on the bar stool and watched him serve himself. He brought a breadbasket filled with blueberry muffins with him when he sat down.

"These muffins are the best," I said between bites.

"Thanks," he answered. "I've always loved breakfast best. That's why hosting a bed and breakfast is no big deal to me."

I thought about that as I buttered another muffin, and wondered about his past—his childhood, not the day when his life changed on 9/11.

"Where did you grow up, Jeff?" I asked.

"I was born in a small town in East Tennessee and attended college at the University of Tennessee."

"I understand you were related to Melissa's husband."

"Bob Williams was my mother's oldest brother."

At the name "Bob" my senses perked up. There had been a Bob in my dream. Of that I was certain. Most of the time, my dreams are formless and shapeless. The one last night held a definite reality to it, almost as if I knew the main characters—Bob, Lizzy, and Henry.

My heart nearly exploded in my chest. I choked on the bite of muffin.

My dream had been about this place. This house.

As the realization raced through my mind, I almost felt the hair lift on the nape of my neck. My dream had been about the Chadwick mansion and little Grace was mentioned. Grace, who was now a ghost. How could this be?

My shoulders tightened. I had someone who could explain it to me. He was sitting next to me at the island bar calmly eating his breakfast. But I didn't dare ask him if he could read dreams. Jeff had failed to send the little ghost home. Maybe his powers weren't that great. And the thought of him reading my mind was appalling —like a complete invasion of privacy.

I put the half-eaten muffin down on the plate and pushed the plate away. I couldn't eat any more.

"Is there something wrong?" Jeff asked.

I could read the concern in his eyes and longed to tell him—to unburden my insecurities and fears and let him enfold me in his arms. But that was a no-go. He had been told to take care of me, but not the way I wanted. I was a silly girl, after all, given to getting into trouble. Note the bad judgment call when I went sledding with Eric.

"Oh, I didn't sleep too well last night." I lied. I'd slept like a baby and even remembered my dreams.

"I'm sorry."

I shrugged. "Nothing you can do. I'm still getting used to things around here."

That was an understatement!

So I watched Jeff finish his meal while I sipped my coffee, fanaticizing about him in the worst, shameful way.

Mr. and Mrs. Martin arrived in the dining room a few minutes after nine. I served them coffee right away, and Jeff brought Mr. Martin the *Wall Street Journal*, which he immediately opened and began to read.

I soon gathered this was an everyday occurrence for Mr. Martin, but probably on most days, he suffered his wife's gossiping in silence. With me waiting on them, Mrs. Martin had someone to talk to. She didn't have to depend upon breaking through the thin piece of newsprint barrier her husband put up to avoid her.

"Did you sleep well?" I asked when I served fresh fruit in crystal compote dishes.

"Well, yes I did, dear, until I heard our little ghost."

Mrs. Martin hadn't been scared at all, and in fact, relished the chance to take part in a paranormal experience. I found it distressing that little Grace was still crying, and my heart twisted as I heard about her deep moans of sadness.

Jeff entered the dining room with plates of omelets and country ham as Mrs. Martin was saying, "You should really see about getting a psychic medium in here to see about that ghost. Not all your guests will find it as exciting as I do."

I glanced at Jeff, and we exchanged knowing looks. "We like our ghost," Jeff said in his deep voice. "I believe she's put us among the tourist attractions in Old Louisville."

"Well, she's such a sad little thing," Mrs. Martin said. "I feel so sorry for her."

I felt sorry for Grace too, but didn't reveal that when *I* heard her, she'd been laughing. I still wanted Jeff to try to help her. He'd said he couldn't do it, but maybe he hadn't tried hard enough. I was determined to ask him again about the ghost when the time was right.

But it wasn't right the rest of the day. The Martins left for their daughter's house, saying they'd return around eight o'clock. I busied myself cleaning their suite. With Corey on vacation, Jeff didn't complain about me stepping in to take her place.

A little after two o'clock, I sat down on the top step of the grand staircase. I wanted to catch my breath, but more than that, I wanted to soak up the atmosphere of the house in the daylight. Defused winter sunshine streamed through the panes of leaded glass that flanked the wood front door. I was alone upstairs, unless Grace was somewhere around, but I didn't see or hear her.

Old houses have a way of creaking and sighing, whether it's because of the wind or simply with old age. I couldn't guess. But I listened to the creaks and sighs, thinking no wonder people imagined they heard ghosts in such places. The Victorian house had a spooky feel to it, but I was beginning to like it, growing comfortable with it. Almost as if I'd known these old pieces of furniture and antiques sometime long ago.

And then I heard a door slam.

"You bastard!"

Angry footfalls approached below me. I sensed the energy of the person coming toward me, and it was a hostile one. Then he came in sight, stomping down the hallway, throwing on his overcoat.

"Eric!" I called from my top step.

He turned and glared at me. "Thanks for telling on me."

I stood up and took a step downward. "What do you mean?"

"Thanks for telling Jeff I kissed you. He fired me!"

"What?" My hand flew to my mouth. "I did no such thing! I didn't tell Jeff anything about our sledding trip."

Eric laughed. "How did he know I kissed you?"

I shook my head, not saying a word, but taking a good guess. *Melissa.*

"How was I to know the Chadwick's precious love child, the little bastard, was off limits?" he said with such contempt.

I came all the way down the stairs. "I don't know what you're talking about."

Yet, his words appalled me. *Love child. Bastard.* I was none of those things. Maybe technically it was true, but I had more self-worth than that. Didn't I? Why should I be condemned by the accident of my birth? And who was Eric, a hired handyman, to judge me?

I straightened my shoulders and jutted out my chin. "Maybe Jeff was right to fire you," I said. "In fact, I'm glad he did."

For a moment, I feared Eric would strike me, but he didn't, even though his eyes blazed with fury.

"Do you think I care about this stinking place?" he asked with a snarl. "This is a crap job. You'll figure it out someday once this place has lured you in and ruined your life."

With that parting shot, Eric jerked open the door and stormed out of the house. I grabbed the edge of the wooden door and watched him tramp down the front steps, icy from the Christmas Eve snowfall. He slipped on the bottom stair and almost fell. I suppressed a giggle. It wouldn't be right to laugh at him. Glancing back to see me at the door, Eric tossed me the bird.

Classic gesture, I thought with a snicker as I softly shut the door.

I was glad Eric was gone. It seemed like negative energy had been sucked out of the house with his departure.

CHAPTER SIXTEEN

I turned to find Jeff watching me. He stood near the Christmas tree by the main staircase.

"I should have fired him long ago," Jeff said quietly.

I looked down at my feet quickly and then up again. "I hope it wasn't because of yesterday. I went with him willingly."

"I know."

His words felt like an indictment, almost as if he was disappointed in me. Well, I was disappointed in myself. Jeff had nothing on me there.

"Melissa hired him," he went on to explain. "Sometimes she wasn't the best judge of people."

Subconsciously, I reached for the antique locket, but it wasn't around my neck. I'd been halfway searching for it upstairs, even though I knew I lost it at the park. Did Jeff know it too? If he was such a great psychic medium, he'd know everything, wouldn't he?

My nerves flared. Our standoff continued. Neither one of us spoke. It was almost as if we wanted to speak, but were both afraid to open up. *Why?* I sensed that if I talked freely to Jeff, my problems might be easily solved. But I was too stubborn or too untrusting to open up. After all, where had it gotten me in the past?

"You don't need me for a while, do you?" I stepped away from the door. "I think I need to take a little drive to clear my head."

He dropped his gaze and turned toward the back of the house. "Sure. Go ahead. But be back before dark. You don't know these streets."

"You sound like my mother," I couldn't help saying.

He turned to face me. "No, this is me talking. Not a spirit."

Concern flashed in his blue eyes that were softened by his caring. I felt the strong vibes he sent. They connected us, even though I tried to avoid them. It was hard to ignore whatever there was between us. I knew someday it had to be explored, but today I felt too raw and insecure. Today was not the time.

I drove back to Cherokee Park and Dog Hill where I parked and walked the mushy, muddy hill, not suitable anymore for sledding. Of course, I didn't find the locket. What did I expect? It was lost in the muck underfoot. And I deserved to lose it as punishment for lacking good judgment. Why couldn't I ever learn to read bad people like Eric? Was it my fatal flaw? Or was I too much like my birth mother? She'd gotten pregnant with me by a jerk that had deserted her.

After searching the hill, I drove back to the Barnes and Noble and browsed the shelves of new age, metaphysical books. I found one, bought it, and took it to the coffee shop. With a hot cup of mocha java in front of me, I sat down at a table to look through the book.

Jeff had said I was psychic. I wanted to know what that meant.

The first thing I learned is that "metaphysical" means, "that which is beyond the physical." It's estimated that humans are ninety-eight percent metaphysical, meaning mental, emotional, and spiritual.

There was a whole chapter on "trust," being able to trust your psychic abilities, but in the beginning verifying them with others to help you know if what you hear or see is right or wrong. Others, like other psychics, I guessed. Someone like Jeff.

I took a deep breath when I read that, because it validated my belief that talking to Jeff could straighten out a lot of things.

But it came down to that word, didn't it? Did I *trust* Jeff enough to expose my greatest fears? Or even simply to admit I'd lost Melissa's treasured locket?

The chapter also talked about the fear of losing control as you explore your newfound gifts. Most people don't open up to their psychic awareness because of fear. It noted that a person must discern this fear. That fear limits the ability to connect with the spirit world that will come to you during your dreamtime.

So, was the dream I experienced about the Chadwick house a manifestation of the spirit world? Were guides or angels trying to tell me something? Would Jeff understand my dream if I revealed it to him?

It was good to know that psychic awareness comes to people in dreams, intuition, and even thoughts. The book said we took it for granted. I wondered about that—about those déjà vu moments that sometimes crop up in our lives when we sense we've been there and done that.

Then I read about cell memory—the déjà vu moments that were actually a body's reaction to memories of past lives. I scoffed at that idea. The concept of reincarnation was foreign to me. I didn't believe it.

I didn't want to believe it.

When I returned to the bed and breakfast before six o'clock, I went into the back of the house and found Jeff busy in the kitchen.

"Good! I'm glad you're back," he said. "Can you help me by setting the dining room table?"

"Sure" I threw him a questioning glance as I hung up my coat.

"We have new guests who have just arrived from Oregon. The wife is pregnant and is too tired to go out for dinner."

I set my purse and Barnes and Noble bag at the end of the butcher-block island. "What are you fixing?"

"I told them I could fix my specialty—breakfast." He gave me a grin. "They didn't seem to mind."

I savored our companionship of the moment. It was much like working with others on the wait-staff at Eggs-to-Go. We had a job to do, and we did it as a team.

"Same dishes as this morning?"

"Yes, you know where to find them."

I set the table and came back into the kitchen for a pitcher of water. I was pouring ice water into glasses when the guests arrived. They were the Hendersons from Portland. The husband was in Louisville on business and didn't want to leave his pregnant wife at home. Mrs. Henderson was only four months along but had been troubled with bouts of morning sickness. The long flight from the coast with the layovers and security checks had worn her out.

Jeff served plates of hot omelets, cheese grits, and sausage. I brought in a basket of blueberry muffins. When I went back to pick up the pot of coffee, I noticed Jeff looking at the book I'd bought. He'd opened the bag, I guess.

He heard me and lifted his gaze. "Learn anything?"

We connected with our eyes. A chill of embarrassment coursed down my spine. Did he think I was questioning his skills?

"A few things," I said.

"Good," he said and thrust the book back into the bag.

We finished the evening without talking. The guests enjoyed

themselves and retired early. About eight-thirty, the Martins returned. Jeff locked the front door after them and sent me to bed. I left the mansion with Jeff sitting in front of the living room fireplace, staring at the burning gas logs and nursing a glass of bourbon, a bottle of Marker's Mark placed by his elbow.

CHAPTER SEVENTEEN

December 28, Present Day

Thursday followed the same routine as the previous day. This time we had four guests to serve for breakfast, but they came downstairs at different times. Mr. Henderson had a meeting downtown, so he and his wife ate before eight o'clock. The Martins followed at nine, Mrs. Martin complaining because she'd not heard the ghost in the night.

But Mrs. Henderson did.

I learned about her sighting of the ghost when I took fresh towels to her room.

"Mrs. Henderson, it's Beth." I knocked on the door. "I've brought you clean towels. May I come in?"

She opened the door for me and returned to her chair in front of the window where she was listening to talk radio. The Henderson's were in the Kentucky Suite, a spacious, bright and sunny room overlooking the handsomely preserved Victorian streetscape of Third Street. As I went into the bathroom, I noticed she was crocheting a blue, baby blanket.

I cleaned the bathroom. Coming and going in and out of the

back rooms several times, I removed wet towels, changed the bed linen, and made the bed. When I was finished, I stopped to say goodbye.

"You're very patient to be able to do that." I nodded to the crochet hooks and the wool blanket forming in her lap.

"Not really," she admitted. "I need something to keep my hands busy. It also takes my mind off of things."

I smiled. "Maybe I need to take it up as a hobby."

We made eye contact, and she smiled back at me. "Did you say your name is Beth?"

I nodded. "Yes."

"Beth, I'm Jenny. Can you sit awhile and keep me company? I mean, is it okay with your employers? I get so lonely with Greg away so much."

I plopped down in the chair across from her. "I suppose it's okay," I said, "since I technically own this place."

Somehow I told her my story, about the whirlwind changes of my life in the past few weeks. Jenny laid her needlework on her lap and listened with rapt attention. Of course, I didn't tell her about Eric or kissing Jeff or anything like that. But I opened up about how odd I felt living in this big house and learning I had a birth mother after all these years.

She shook her head as if she understood. "It makes you wonder about these big, old houses, doesn't it? So much heartache must have taken place in them over the years. Imagine how your grandfather reacted when he learned his only daughter was pregnant."

"I know. People with money can be just a miserable as people who don't have any."

"The presence of the little girl makes me sad," Jenny said without warning.

I sat on the edge of my seat. "What? Have you seen our ghost?"

She acknowledged that she had. "I'm sort of psychic that way. I heard her crying last night and caught a glimpse of white light running along the hallway."

Sitting back in the seat, I felt a twinge of frustration. "I've seen her too," I said in a strained voice.

"You have?"

"Yes, but when I see her, she's happy. She's laughing."

"Really?"

I answered with a small nod. "I think I'm the only one who sees her that way. Even the other guest, Mrs. Martin, heard her crying the other night."

"You must be special to the ghost," Jenny said.

I drew my eyebrows together. "How's that?"

"There must be something about you she relates to. Maybe because you're young."

"But you're not any older than me," I objected.

"I'm twenty-four."

"And I'm twenty-five."

"Well, that can't be it then." She tapped her finger on the arm of her chair. "I don't know what it is, but it's something. I bet if you think long enough, you'll figure it out."

"I don't know." I shrugged my shoulders.

"Maybe you should meditate about it. You might get your answer then."

Standing up, I agreed to try meditation. Jenny wished me luck as I left the room. I didn't tell her I didn't know how to meditate.

When the guests were upstairs, the house shut up for the night, and Jeff in his carriage house apartment, I returned to the library. Jeff had given me a key to the back door. I used it to slip inside, turning on only the back hall light. In the library, I sat in the dark in front of a stone cold fireplace, the one with Grace's portrait hanging on the wall over the mantle.

A security light in the courtyard outside cast a glow through the white, sheer curtains of the back window. It illuminated the portrait enough so I saw Grace's blond curls, white frilly dress, and sweet innocent smile. I'd poured a glass of red wine, thinking it would relax me, and sipped from the stemmed glass as I stared up at the painting.

Grace's image didn't move, but I willed it to. Not knowing how to meditate, I settled for quiet, darkness, deep breathing, and trying to blank out my thoughts. I wasn't too good at the latter, my mind whirling with questions, seeking answers.

Sometime after the grandfather clock struck midnight, I heard a tiny giggle. I put the glass of wine on the end table and sat up.

I heard it again, this time nearer.

And then I saw a film of silver light hovering near the portrait.

"Grace?" My accent startled me. It had an Irish lilt to it, not my own Southern Kentucky twang. The hairs at the nape of my neck seemed to stand on end.

The laughter grew louder. The image flickered. I felt light-headed, yet I could see the child's body take shape in front of me. She opened her arms to me. I rose and took a step toward her, my own hand extended toward hers.

"Let me help you," I said, my voice strained. Then a feeling of shame washed over me, and I felt tears well up in my eyes. "I'm so sorry!"

She smiled at me, holding out her hand. I reached for it, wishing I were more psychic, that I could actually speak to her, that I could send her to heaven where she belonged.

In my head, I heard the words, "It's not your fault."

My skin tingled as sweat formed on my upper lip. I gulped a few short, fast breaths.

"What do you mean?"

"It's not your fault," I heard again in my head.

"Grace, I'm sorry!"

Suddenly, the overhead lights in the room blazed on. The ghost of little Grace vanished as quickly as she'd appeared.

"Beth, is that you in here?" Jeff strode into the library. "Are you okay?"

I didn't look at him, because I had collapsed to the floor sobbing, hiding my face in my hands.

"What's wrong?" I sensed Jeff kneeling next to me. "Are you hurt?" The anxiety rose in his voice.

"I saw her," I blubbered. "I saw the ghost!"

He sat down on the floor and took me into his arms, cradling me, comforting me as if I was a child. "It's okay. She can't hurt you."

"She told me it wasn't my fault," I said, eyes wet and nose running. "What does it mean, Jeff? You're a medium. You should know what it means."

"Did you hear her?

"In my head."

He hugged me close, and I felt as if I belonged there in his arms, his warm and vibrant body shielding mine. Not saying a word, Jeff kissed the top of my head and pulled me nearer to him. I wanted to stay there forever. Being sheltered in his embrace felt so good, even though it was wrong.

A sharp pang of fear stabbed me in the gut. Melissa wouldn't want us together like this. She wouldn't expect that of us. She'd instructed Jeff to take care of me.

So many feelings were rushing through my body, confusing my mind. I didn't know what to do, even though I longed to stay in Jeff's arms and never leave.

But I couldn't. For one thing, Jeff should have answers for me, yet he wasn't providing them. I sensed he was avoiding my questions.

Pulling away, I sat up and focused on his face. Wiping the tears away with the back of my hand, I gazed at the dark worry in his eyes. "Jeff, why can't you send her to the light? Like in the movie?"

"This isn't a movie, Beth. I told you she isn't ready to go home."

"Why not?" I cried. "Even though I hear her laughter, I sense a tremendous sadness about her. Something horrible happened to her, and we've got to help her."

"I know she's sad," Jeff said, breaking eye contact and looking up at Grace's portrait.

"Then why haven't you done more to help her?" I was desperate. "I don't buy it that she's not ready to go. You can help her. I know you can."

His face flushed with emotion. I didn't know with what kind. His shoulders tensed. Jeff uncoupled himself from me and stood up. I watched him run his fingers through his black hair as he stared at the portrait.

"I'm afraid to try, Beth," he said in a voice wracked with agony.

Had I heard him right? I scrambled to my feet. "What?"

His back was to me. We both gazed at the child's portrait. "I know it doesn't make sense."

"Tell me," I whispered.

The room pulsed with the tension between us and with an unseen energy that threatened to overcome us. I was drawn to him, as I've never before been drawn to another human being.

"I'm afraid of what I'll find out." His words came out in a despairing gasp. "I've never explored all the possibilities of my psychic gifts. I've been too damn afraid."

His revelation was a crucial one. I sensed that it had much to do with his whole essence as a human being. He had hidden himself away in this place after 9/11, taking care of other people, but never himself. Had his trauma during that horrific day in 2001 done this to him? Did he have posttraumatic stress disorder? Or was it something more? Something more profound?

"Oh, Jeff, we're a fine pair, aren't we?" I gave him a tiny grin. "Haunted by our past, we're afraid of the future."

"That is more true than you know," he said with an anguish that touched his eyes.

I reached out and took his hand. It was clammy. He looked down at our clasped hands and sighed.

"Oh, Beth."

And then I was in his arms again, frantically kissing him. His mouth plundered mine with a raw sexual desire that had nothing to do with anyone's past. *Screw, Melissa!* Screw everything and everybody but this man in my arms. This man who was making love to me in a fusty old library with the ghosts of long-dead ancestors staring down from plaster walls.

He must have felt their presence and didn't want them watching us, because he picked me up in his arms. "Oh, Jeff," I whispered, my body seething with desire.

"Let's go to my apartment." His words were a plea, a question... a demand.

I put my arms around his neck and buried my face into his shoulder. "Yes, take me," I said.

Take me in more ways than one.

I ached for Jeff. I ached for him as a woman aches for a man. In the intimacy of his darkened bedroom, he reached out for me, drawing me close. Wrapping his arms around my scantily clad body, he splayed his hands on my back and shoulders, pulling me closer to his bare chest. We wore only our underwear—bra, panties and boxer shorts. It seemed sort of pointless when all we wanted to do was strip each other naked and get at it fast and furious.

But Jeff had said, "Let's go slow. Let's savor the moment."

Savoring was good I'd thought until my body responded to his with such a fire that I thought my heart was going to explode.

He lowered his mouth to mine, nipped my lower lip, and then kissed it tenderly. I parted my lips to respond to him.

As we kissed, I felt his hands fumble with the clasp of my bra. In a moment, it was released. The pressure on my breasts relaxed. Jeff slipped the straps off my shoulders and dropped the constricting garment to the floor. Now totally free from constraint, I pushed my breasts up against him, feeling the hardness of his chest and the tickling of his chest hairs.

Jeff groaned. I bit my lower lip, my actions driving me into turmoil. His hands sought my bottom and pulled me even closer, up against his fully erect penis. I reached for his hips, and we danced like that together, both wanting, our mouths insistent, our bodies demanding.

Our underwear came off.

He backed me up, and we tumbled onto his king-size bed. Jeff broke my fall and didn't allow his full weight to collapse on me. The action dissolved any restraint we pretended to have. He explored my body with his hands and tongue, making me twist beneath him with passion. I gasped with desire as he descended, kissing me below my belly button, and I trailed my fingernails softly over the flesh of his strong back.

Gently parting my thighs, he kissed me there in my private place. I was slick with wanting him. And as his tongue entered me, I writhed with the painful pleasure of his touch. Jeff was taking me to places I'd never been. I loved him for it. I loved him as my lust overcame me. I cried out his name and shuddered, hanging on to his back during the waves of pure delight washing over me.

Jeff savored the moment. Letting me enjoy coming down from my climax. Limp. Exhausted. Yet, I could tell he was fully ready, needing his own release. He threw a leg over me, prying between my thighs with his penis. It was hot. I was hot. My eyes flew open, and I saw the scorching look in Jeff's eyes.

"I need you," he said in a voice thick with passion.

I cupped his face in my hands and pulled his lips towards mine. His need I could satisfy.

I shifted under him, helping him find the spot. Then I lifted my legs, tightening them around his hips. He slid inside me, filling me up, holding himself at bay as if to relish the moment to its fullest.

"Beth!"

His cry pierced my heart. I wanted to hold him safe inside me forever.

Then he began to move within me. Slowly at first and then growing in momentum. I held him for dear life. Loving it because he needed me as no other man before him had ever admitted.

Loving him as I'd loved no other man.

By giving of myself there was no going back. Our lives were intertwined just as our bodies.

And when it was all over, when we were so tired we couldn't move, Jeff wrapped me in his arms again, and we lay there in his bed finding it hard to move. Or to talk. It was enough to be there together. To take comfort from each other's physical being. Sometime after that I heard the rhythm of his relaxed breath signaling he was asleep.

Peaceful. Content. I fell asleep too.

CHAPTER EIGHTEEN

December 29, Present Day

I awoke in Jeff's bed. Sunshine streamed through his bedroom window. He was gone, his side rumpled and cold.

Alarmed, I checked the clock on his nightstand. It was ten o'clock, and breakfast should be long over. He'd let me sleep in. I stretched and wiggled between the sheets, happy at the thought of his thoughtfulness. Pulling the covers up to my neck and snuggling under them, I gazed at the ceiling and relived our night of lovemaking.

Perhaps it was his age or his experience level, but I'd never made love like that in my whole life. Thoroughly sated, tremendously satisfied, I sighed at the memory of his kisses and at the way he moaned with excitement when he came. I had to smile remembering my shouts during my climax. God, it had been such an overwhelming experience, and I longed to do it again.

And again.

Without any thought to correctness or consequences.

But I did think about what we'd done, and slowly shame seeped through my body leaving me cold and weary. It wasn't guilt, for I had no remorse because of our fabulous sex. Jeff was a single man. I, a single woman. Nothing wrong there.

Yet, in my psyche, there had always been sadness and an underpinning of shame, as if I am a bad person, inherently so. Probably it stemmed from never knowing my real parents, from always trying to make my adopted parents happy, and then failing miserably on so many occasions. I had no clue. I'm not a psychologist. All I wanted to do was revel in my memories of the night with Jeff and enjoy whatever came from it.

When I got out of bed, I found I ached inside. Ah, I celebrated the feeling of soreness, because it provided proof of our lovemaking. There was something comforting in that reminder. Something tangible that I knew would stay with me for a long time.

I showered in Jeff's bathroom and wrapped my hair into a turban with his towel. I found a white T-shirt and put it on without any underpants. I took liberties that a day earlier I would never have taken. It felt good. As if I belonged here. As if this was where I was to stay.

Jeff came back near eleven carrying muffins and coffee. "You're up," he said setting the goodies down on the coffee table in front of the TV.

I was sitting on the leather sofa, my legs crossed, drying my hair with the towel. I looked up and smiled. We connected right away with a smile and a deep, longing look. I knew it was going to be okay. That something in my life had changed for the better.

"I'm sorry I didn't help you this morning." I accepted the hot mug of coffee and cradled it in my hands.

"I didn't need you," he said and then added, "there."

The way he said it, and his knowing gaze set my insides ablaze. I ached in the places already sore. Where did he need me again? In bed? With him? Could we make a relationship out of whatever bond we felt? Out of one night of good sex?

"Yet, I should have gotten up to help." I could be gallant even though I'd enjoyed sleeping in.

"Corey came back today," he told me and sat down next to me on the sofa.

The simple act of my knee touching his thigh sent my senses flaring. Over the rim of the coffee mug, I saw his eyes light and then darken.

"Oh, God, Beth," he said in an agonizing whisper, "I want you again."

"I want you too."

The simple admission was all that it took for Jeff to lift the mug from my hands, set it on the coffee table, and push me back on the sofa.

He hovered over me, his hands exploring under my T-shirt. "What is it about you?" he asked with a seriousness I didn't understand. "Why do I feel as if I've known you all my life? Why do I feel like we belong together?"

"You're the psychic," I reminded him.

"I'm just a man at this moment, Beth," he said as his lips found mine. "Just a man."

All thoughts flew out of my head. I simply reacted with my heart and my soul as any woman would react with the man she loved.

By three o'clock I'd finally struggled up to my apartment, showered for the second time that day, and dressed. Finding that I was hungrier than I'd ever been in my life, I threw on a coat and walked across the courtyard into the old house.

Corey was in the kitchen polishing silver serving pieces. "Hey," she greeted me with a smile.

"Hi, Corey." I was honestly glad to see her. "Did you have a good time off?"

"Oh, it was nothing special," she said with a shrug. "But it was good to sleep in."

"Tell me about it," I commented dryly, thinking of my own recent experience.

"What have you been up to?"

"Nothing much." I felt the warmth of the blush in my cheeks. "I've been standing in for you. I hope you don't find the rooms too much of a mess."

"One couple left this morning," she told me, "and I've already cleaned their suite. We have two more reservations for the weekend."

"What about the older couple? The grandparents?"

"They went off to visit their grandchildren this morning. I think the man is tired of the whole thing and wants to go home."

From what I'd seen of the Martins that sounded right to me. I made a ham sandwich from fixings in the refrigerator, bypassed the Coke, and poured myself a glass of water. I sat down at the island to eat it.

"I've been invited to this off-campus party tonight," Corey said. "I don't want to go alone and wondered if you'd like to come with me. You can meet people. I thought you might enjoy that especially if you sign up for classes."

I considered her request between bites. Not particularly a partying person, I would rather stay home and party with Jeff. Yet, something told me I shouldn't take this fledgling relationship for granted. I didn't need to be a clingy, desperate woman like I'd always been, especially since Jeff was older. He might not think that trait attractive.

"What time?"

"It starts at nine. I can pick you up at eight-thirty."

"Okay," I said and took a sip of water. I did want to belong and fit into my new life. "Where is Jeff, by the way?"

"All he said was that he needed to clear his head and would be back soon."

"Okay," I said again.

What did he need to clear his head about?

Me?

Us?

Of course, that was it. Was he having regrets about what happened? Because of Melissa?

Away from him, my insecurities arose full-throated. I choked them down, but not well enough. My insides quivered because of my own doubts.

Did an *us* even exist? Good God. Was I being presumptions like so many times before? Jumping the gun when I needed to step back, take a breath and go slow?

Yes, going to Corey's party was just the thing for me. I needed to clear my head too. Establish my own independence. Because so much that could go wrong *had* gone wrong with my lovers in the past. I had a hard time trusting myself, let alone any man who came into my life.

After cleaning up my plate and glass, I told Corey I'd be ready at eight-thirty. Then I climbed the steps to my apartment to while away the hours until it was time to leave. Signing up for classes would do me good. The need to study and write papers would take away the boredom and uncertainty that hung over me at the moment. Sitting at the desk, I pulled up the University of Louisville on the Internet and surfed through the site looking for registration dates and class schedules.

Later that afternoon, my mom called from her sister's house. They were going out for dinner soon, and she wanted to talk to me before they left. We chatted about my college plans, and I told her about going with Corey to a party tonight. She wished me well, and said she heard the happiness in my voice.

Was she psychic too?

We hung up with me admitting to myself that I was happy. My mom was right. Never a good one to hide my emotions, I couldn't even hide them in my tone of voice hundreds of miles away from my mom. I smiled at that thought and cherished my memories of last night. Being with Jeff made me happy. I didn't know why. It just did. That was enough, wasn't it?

Jeff hadn't returned home by eight o'clock. It worried me, but then I told myself I had no control over him. Just because we'd slept together, he didn't owe me anything, even knowledge of his whereabouts. I thought about texting him that I was going out with Corey, but I'd never texted him. He had my cell phone number, and I had his, but texting seemed presumptions on my part. What if he didn't care where I was going?

See how those old insecurities reared their ugly heads?

I put on clean blue jeans and my ankle-length boots that made me look as if I was wearing real cowboy boots under my jeans. I chose a maroon Henley shirt with lacy patterns and geometric figures stitched around the neck. The shirt emphasized my trim figure, and the low neck revealed my collarbones. I felt sexy enough to go to a party where I hoped to make a good impression on people who may become my classmates and friends.

When eight-thirty arrived, so did Corey. I slung on my coat and ran downstairs to meet her.

CHAPTER NINETEEN

Corey drove us down Third Street toward the U of L campus. Not sure of my way around town, I didn't know exactly where she took me, but the party was held in a small, white house that was perfect for college students to share. We went in the back door, through the kitchen, and into a crowded living room filled with sofas and chairs that had seen better days. "Just Give Me a Reason" by Pink was blasting from a surround sound system.

A bunch of kids stood outside on the front porch in the cold weather drinking beer and smoking cigarettes. Corey introduced me to a blond-haired boy with a girl balanced on his knee as if he was Santa Claus. Her ears were lined with diamond studs and the guy had an earring in the lobe of each ear.

"Glad to meet you," the boy said extending a hand. I took it, noticing a tattoo running up his arm, and was happy to withdraw my hand after shaking his.

His girlfriend gave me speculative look, sizing up the new competition, I guessed. She didn't offer me her hand, but sipped her white wine instead, glaring at me over the rim of her glass.

I didn't remember their names. And I was suddenly sorry I'd come.

"Do you want something to drink?" Corey asked.

"Sure." I thought better of asking for wine given my last experience. I didn't need to be dizzy after drinking half a glass, and I didn't like the taste of beer. "Where's the bar? I'll go grab something for us both. What do you want?"

"Whatever kind of beer they've got," Corey replied.

The table in the dining room was laden with chips and dips. Bottles of bourbon and vodka lined one corner of it along with two-liter bottles of Coke and club soda for mixers. I filled a red plastic cup with a handful of ice from a bag housed in a cooler and then poured Coke over the cubes, thinking of Jeff and his opinion of my Coke addiction. I pulled an icy Corona Light from another cooler on the floor and popped the cap using the bottle opener tied to the handle of the cooler

Returning to the living room, I found Corey talking to a couple of guys—one a political science major and the other a journalism student. They were hotly debating politics, throwing out words like "conservative," "liberal," "Tea Party," and "political correctness." I listened to their debate, smiling faintly and acting as if I understood what they were saying.

And asked myself if I'd ever fit in.

We lasted an hour with those guys, and then Corey led the way back into the dining room for another beer. I freshened my Coke, wondering how long Corey planned to stay.

"Well, look who's here." Someone grabbed my upper left arm and spun me around.

"Eric!"

"Fancy running into the Chadwick's precious love child."

"Let go of me!" I jerked my arm free and rubbed it.

He leered at me. "Ain't got your lover boy here to defend you."

Corey inserted herself between us, but I could feel my face flush hot because of his remark. What did he know about Jeff and me? Or was he simply guessing? My stomach churned, and I felt myself violated somehow.

"Back off, Eric," Corey snapped. "What are you doing here?"

"Party crashing," he said with a cocky smile. "Same as everybody else."

She shoved him in the chest, and he moved back a step. "Well, find yourself someone else to hang with. We're busy."

"I betcha you are." His upper lip curled in a snarl, and his eyes narrowed.

"Go on. Get out of our way!"

Eric bowed with a flourish of his hand almost like a court jester of old, but let us scoot past. We ducked into a front bedroom with a bed piled high with coats.

"You okay?" Corey asked, her gaze seeking mine.

"Yes," I said a bit breathlessly. "He just startled me."

"Jeff told me he was fired. Guess he's carrying a grudge."

I nodded. "I suppose so."

"Well, stick with me. He's all talk and bluster."

I wanted to ask when we were leaving but just smiled weakly instead. The living room was hot and crowded when we went back into it. I found the crush of people even more oppressive. Corey led me over to introduce me to another group of students. I said hello, but then stood on the outskirts of the circle with my arms crossed, subconsciously forming a barrier between others and myself in the group.

A girl named Sarah was majoring in marketing just like I wanted to do. Eventually, I started talking to her. We hit it off and separated ourselves to chat in the kitchen where it was a little cooler. She gave me some tips about professors and classes, so my night wasn't totally wasted.

Near eleven o'clock, the flip cup game started.

I'd seen the game at other parties. It was a relay race between two teams drinking a measured amount of beer from plastic cups.

The team that finished drinking and flipping all its cups first was the winner.

Someone had cleared off the dining room table except for a row of eight red plastic cups on each side of the table. Sixteen players sorted themselves out, each in various stages of sobriety, and lined up with eight to a team. The journalism student poured beer into each cup.

Then the crowd started clapping and chanting, "Flip cup! Flip cup!"

The first two contestants held up their cups saluting each other. "Cheers!"

They touched their cups to the table, saluted each other again, and touched the table a second time with their cups. That was the signal for them both to start drinking, chugging down the beer as fast as they could drink it.

The game got its name from the next part. Once the cup was emptied, the contestant placed it on the edge of the table and tried to flip it over with a flick of a finger. Not easy to do, this part of the game led to quite a few hoots and hollers and shrieks of encouragement. Since this was a relay race, the next person in line couldn't start drinking until the prior person had flipped the cup.

Drinking and flipping continued down the line. The competition intensified. Finally, Corey's team finished first and won. Then the losing team challenged them to a rematch, and they played another game. This time Corey's competition won.

I watched from a safe distance, noticing kids getting buzzed. Shrill shrieks of laughter filled the room. There was a competitive energy pulsating around the table as more of the contestants let go of their inhibitions and the noise rose to a fever pitch.

The drunken scene appalled me. This wasn't my idea of fun. My mom had called me "an old soul," and I had always guessed she meant my natural reserve and shyness. I had no desire to lose control of myself in a situation like this.

"One more! One more!" some guy yelled. "Let's decide the winner. Best two out of three!"

At that moment, Santa Claus rushed from the room with his hand over his mouth. "Oh, my God! I'm going to be sick!"

That left Corey's team with only seven players. She turned to me. "Beth, come on and play!"

I shook my head no.

"Don't be a spoilsport." Someone shoved me from behind toward the table.

"Ah, come on, Beth. I didn't think you were a chicken!"

If someone other than Corey had called me "chicken," I wouldn't have agreed to play. But she was my friend, and she looked as if she was having a good time. I didn't want to disappoint her. I wanted to fit in.

"Okay! Okay!" I took my place at the end of the line.

The game started again, this time with me dreading every flip of a cup. When my turn came, my heart pumped with urgency. We were ahead, but not by much. I tapped the cup on the table like I'd seen the others do, picked it up, and drank.

God, how I hate beer.

I spilled more out the sides of my mouth and down my neck than I actually drank. Yet, managing to empty the cup, I put it on the edge of the table and flicked it. The stupid thing skittered across the table. Everyone was shouting at me. My opponent was trying to flip his cup too. I grabbed mine and tried again, this time successfully turning it upside down on the table.

We won.

I didn't feel like much of a hero.

In fact, I felt sticky and sick from the beer.

"You did it!" Corey congratulated me. "Wasn't that fun?"

"Oh, yes," I agreed with a big dose of sarcasm in my voice. "I'm a mess. Where's the bathroom so I can clean up?"

After throwing cold water over my face to rinse it clean, I

wiped myself dry with someone's damp bath towel hanging next to the sink. Then I went to the bathroom. There wasn't any toilet paper. When I stood up, I was dizzy. I staggered a step and caught myself from falling by clutching the doorknob. Fresh air, I thought. *I need fresh air.*

Coming out of the bathroom, I stumbled into the living room. Corey wasn't there. I needed to go home. Where was she?

"Corey's gone upstairs with a guy."

I turned at the sound of Eric's voice. His face swam in front of me. "Oh?"

"You know how that is." He winked at me.

What was that supposed to mean? Was he telling me Corey had gone to have sex with a guy?

Everything seemed to be moving in slow motion, especially me. My brain was fuzzy. I took a deep breath trying to get my bearings. All I knew was that I didn't want to be here any longer. I wanted to go home.

Home.

I wanted to go back to the Chadwick Bed and Breakfast. It *was* my home. I wanted to go back there and tell Jeff I suddenly felt like I belonged.

I must have said I wanted to go home, because Eric offered me a ride.

"I don't want to go with you," I said to Eric, slurring my words. "I don't trust you."

"C'mon, Beth. Don't be that way. I'm okay. I'm not going to hurt you. Just drive you home. That's all."

Home. I so wanted to go home and leave this nightmare of a party. Corey was upstairs with a guy. I didn't want to interfere.

Eric stood there, smiling, his eyes earnestly boring into mine. I could trust him, couldn't I?

"Okay. Please take me home." I felt my heart palpitating. "I'm feeling really, really sick."

Eric grasped my upper arm to steady me. "Let's get you home. You must have had too much to drink."

Together we walked through the living room. The crowd had thinned out. I tripped, but Eric caught me and put his arm around my shoulder. I could walk better then.

He helped me into his car, drew the seatbelt over my lap, buckled it, and shut the door. I'd forgotten my coat. I thought to tell Eric, but didn't say it. Instead, I lay my head against the cold glass of the window and shut my eyes.

The last thing I remember wondering was how I got so drunk on such a small amount of beer.

CHAPTER TWENTY

Thursday, March 27, 1890
The Falls City Hall
1126 Market Street, Louisville, Kentucky

Because of the rain, Nurse walked us to the trolley stop on Fourth Street under a huge, black umbrella, and put Miss Grace and me on a newfangled electric trolley car for our trip to dancing lessons. Henry would pick us up in a carriage, Nurse told us, because she didn't want us riding a streetcar after dark. Rain fell, but not the pounding rain of earlier in the day. It was five o'clock.

By the time we reached the Falls City Hall on Market Street, the rain was falling harder. Hot and humid, gloomy clouds hung low and oppressive. I was tired of the rain, and I knew Miss Grace was too.

"I don't want to go," she'd said to Nurse earlier. "Don't make Lizzy and me go." But her governess would not let Grace beg off, as much as to have time for herself as for concern about Grace's social education.

Yet, once Grace saw me dressed in my Sunday best and learned I was meeting Bob there, she changed her mind. "You've got to be there," she told me. "You never know what Bob has planned for you."

She was a romantic, Miss Grace. With a dreamy light in her eyes, she always thought the best of people, even Nurse, who was basically a selfish busybody. As we neared the three-story, brick assembly hall riding in the cramped, smelly trolley car, Grace caught my excitement. She took my hand as we stepped out into the rain, and we scurried into the front door, past shops closed for the evening, and a staircase leading to the upper two floors. Then we walked down the hall to Miss Rosa App's dancing class located in a large back room.

Filled with fifty to seventy children and their parents, the room was crowded, stuffy, and loud. I found an empty chair, and balanced Grace on my knee until Katie Frazier started playing the piano to quiet the children. Miss App motioned for a young man to be her partner. They demonstrated waltz steps, and then invited the children to join them. Grace hopped up, partnering with another little girl dressed in white organza, and they both practiced as Miss App went from couple to couple instructing.

As usual, I felt out of place, but the other mothers had come to expect that one of the Chadwick's employees would bring Grace. When Mrs. Chadwick was in town, the chore was left to Nurse. And of course, there was no question who took the child when her parents were away. Me. A servant girl from the working class side of town.

Time seemed to drag. I worried about leaving Grace alone in the dancing class but told myself it would be all right. There were plenty of women in the room who would not let anything happen to her. I tapped my booted foot on the wooden floor in time with the piano music and tried to slow my breathing. Would Bob really come? Would he really ask me to marry him?

And then I saw him, hat in hand, standing at the door to the assembly room. He looked drenched from head to foot, but as he smiled at me from across the crowded room, my heart melted. I stood slowly. Uncertain.

Grace saw him too and ran over to me. "There he is, Lizzy! Are you going? You must!" I thought better of it, but Grace's earnest blue eyes persuaded me. "You might never get another chance," she said.

She was right. Bob was leaving tomorrow on his riverboat. Heaven only knew when I'd see him again.

"I'll just talk to him out in the hall. Don't leave. I'll be back to pick you up."

"Go," Grace said, touching my sleeve. "You will be safe."

With her approval, I turned to leave, circling the edge of the dance floor to the front door. My last glimpse of Grace was of her giggling and whispering to the little girl who was her partner.

"You should have come to the back door," I admonished Bob.

"It's locked. 'Sides, I couldn't wait to see you!"

He was so dark and handsome. I trembled with excitement, my lips parting slightly. "I mustn't stay away long."

He winked. "Just long enough."

Bob took my hand and pulled me into the hallway. He kissed me hard, but briefly, tasting of whiskey. "C'mon. Let's get away from here."

I sensed he'd had too much to drink, but I didn't want him to stir up trouble, so took a few steps with him down the hall. "I can't leave Miss Grace," I told him.

"She'll be okay."

I wanted to believe him. In fact, I did believe him, for what could happen to her in the crowded room surrounded by friends? Miss App ran a respectable class. She'd look after Grace.

Bob led me down the hall to the outer door of the building. Light-headed, I hurried after him, feeling safe and secure with my fingers linked with his.

Outside, the rain had let up. "I can't talk to you here," Bob said and tugged my hand to urge me outside.

I felt a sudden alarm. "Where are we going?"

"Across the street. To the saloon."

"I can't go into a saloon! Mrs. Chadwick will fire me."

Something warned me not to go. But he was jerking my hand, and I blindly followed. We were halfway across the street with the hail started to fall.

"Quick! Inside!" Bob ordered.

"I can't!" There was no way I'd step foot into a saloon. Hard pellets of hail stung my shoulders. I feared for our safety. "Let's go back, Bob."

"What are you, chicken? It's just a little hail."

He pulled me into the alley beside the saloon just as the street-lamps went out. Blackness descended upon us like a pall. He shoved me up against the side of the brick building, shielding me with his body. The roof overhang sheltered us. Even though Bob was with me, protecting me, I shook uncontrollably.

"Don't be scared, Lizzy," he whispered in my ear, his voice almost drowned out by the windstorm around us.

And then he kissed me. Intense and passionate. I responded to him, putting our harsh surroundings out of my mind. This was Bob, my true love. He and I were going to marry. He would ask me tonight. Soon.

"God, you're so beautiful, Lizzy. I want you. I mean to have you."

My lower body flooded with warmth. His lips moved over mine, and his hands cupped my face. Then he thrust his knee between my legs, my long skirts entangling my legs and making it impossible for me to move even if I'd wanted to.

Was this what it was like to feel loved? Needed? To experience desire for a man? The questions skittered through my mind as the storm raged, and my heart erupted with love.

I simply reacted to his senseless and mind-numbing kisses, his hot breath against my neck. I forgot about consequences.

When Bob parted my blouse with his fingers, I jerked in response. He touched my naked breasts, and I flinched. *No!* My brain finally registered what had happened, and my eyes flew open. There was a bright glitter in Bob's eyes. I saw it through the blackness that surrounded us when lightening stabbed the night sky.

I squirmed beneath Bob's touches. "No! You mustn't!"

He was frantic with a wildness I'd never seen. His mouth came down upon an exposed nipple. I was appalled when I looked at his black head pressed against my breast and felt his teeth and tongue on my flesh. What was he doing?

What had I done?

"Are you going to marry me, Bob?" I cried frantically.

Did he laugh? I felt the rough, painful edges of the bricks rubbing my back. He pressed against me. Somewhere in my thick mind, I registered what was happening. I'd led him on, and he was unable to stop.

I yanked his hair. "Bob! Answer me!"

His face swam before mine—a gloating, lust-filled gleam igniting his eyes. "Marry you? I'm not the marrying kind."

"What?" I squirmed and tried to shove him away.

But Bob was too strong. He knew it. He knew I was helpless beneath him. "Don't have a conniption fit, Lizzy. I mean to have you."

His words were no longer terms of endearment to my ears. I shuddered at the threat they posed. "No! I'll scream! Get away from me!"

I heard his laugh this time, long and deep. "Who will hear you? Not in this storm."

"You can't! It isn't right."

"It isn't right for you to tease me."

"You're drunk." I tried to make sense of his words and the contempt I saw in his eyes. "You don't mean it!"

"Shut up, bitch!" Then he slapped me across the mouth. My head jerked sideways toward the building, and I felt the rough brick scrape my cheek. His hands were all over me. He was all over me. I shut my eyes as fear rolled through me like the pounding thunder around us. And then I felt my taffeta skirt pushed upward, bunching around my waist. A knee easily separated my stocking-clad legs, and I was shoved against the wall.

When his penis entered my body, I screamed. The winds howled. I knew what was happening even though I was a virgin. I'd seen enough curs on the street to know. Pain seared through me, almost ripping me wide open. And then the horrible thrusts that slammed me against the hard wall, ripping my blouse, were more than I could take.

But what choice did I have? I was in his control. His domination. I felt hot tears of shame on my face. He ravished my neck with his mouth and teeth as the throes of lust overcame him. He grunted at the end. I turned my head away from him, unable to look at him. Unable to think.

He stepped back from me. My skirts were still bunched around my waist. "I told you I had something for you," Bob said with smugness in his voice that turned my stomach.

My head whipped around. "Bastard!" I spit in his face.

He laughed. "See you around, Lizzy, my girl."

My last view of Bob was as he walked out of the alley, his step jaunty and his shoulder swing cocky. The rain had stopped. I tugged down my skirts, and in a mindless motion, smoothed them over and over again with the palms of my hands.

It had happened so fast—maybe in only five minutes while the storm thundered around us. I shook. My knees buckled, and I sank weakly to the cobblestones. What if he'd knocked me up? What if I became pregnant? Lord, what would happen to me then?

An unmarried woman with a child. No one would believe it was rape. And maybe it wasn't. Maybe I had teased him. Maybe it was my fault.

The wind whipped up again, and rain fell in torrents. I was somewhat protected in the alley next to the saloon. No one was coming or going on a night like this.

Thank heavens Miss Grace was safe in the Falls City Hall.

CHAPTER TWENTY-ONE

Thursday, March 27, 1890
Across from the Falls City Hall
Between 8:00 and 8:30 p.m.

Suddenly, the stormy night danced with small, bright blue-green to white flashes of lightning that seemed to touch the ground all around me. I huddled next to the building, terrified, my heart pumping widely and my recent rape emptied from my mind as I felt a fear I'd never felt in my life.

The air smelled of brimstone. Odoriferous. Frightening.

I heard a low, moaning sound, and then the noise of a freight train barreling down upon me. But there were no trains in this part of Market Street. I covered my head with my hands and arms. Whirling dust and debris pelted me. The pressure was intense. At the apex of the horrible windstorm, I despaired of living through it.

And then it was over.

The freight train sound receded, heading toward the river and the opposite Indiana shore. I stood, shaking. My chest hurt, but I thought it was from the fear that had gripped me for those terrifying seconds. I took a step and staggered. Gathering myself, I walked forward through the alley.

Miss Grace!

I stumbled down the alley as fast as I could, dodging fallen bricks and pieces of roof. Remarkably, the rain and hail had vanished. There was a strange silence. I emerged from the alley onto Market Street. A bright moon, blood red because of the strange haze in the air, illuminated the destruction all around me. The three-story Falls City Hall was a pile of rubble.

Miraculously, the building housing the saloon had sheltered me and remained intact, unscathed by the horrific winds. But the hall across the street, the building that had housed the dancing class filled with students and parents, was destroyed.

I ran across the street. Two men stood at the edge of the devastation studying it. One carried a lantern.

"What happened?" I cried.

They turned to stare at me.

"Cyclone," one man said in a dead calm voice that struck my heart with dread.

"Were you in there?" the other asked.

"Yes," I answered, because I had been in there earlier.

"Thank the Lord you made it out."

I nodded, without answering, knowing that my survival had been God's blessing. But I didn't reveal the truth of my ordeal, or that I had been across the street huddling in my shame when the wind spared me.

Now my only concern was Grace. Was she alive under that ruin of fallen bricks, glass, and lumber?

"My employers' daughter was in the dancing class," I said, gasping for breath. "Miss App's class. On the first floor. Women...children."

The two men looked at each other for a brief moment and, in silent agreement, turned toward the fallen debris and crawled one-by-one through a small hole where the stairway once ascended to the upper floors.

I stood there—helpless—trying to block out the unearthly sounds of moaning and crying that came from trapped or dying people in the wreckage. My mind was numbed by the implications of my actions. I should have been inside with Grace, holding her, helping her. Instead, I stood on the outside safe and sound, except for my mortifying disgrace. My selfishness had taken me away from my duty. I was no better than the self-centered governess or the venal man I had thought I loved.

The temperature had dropped. I was shivering, hugging my body with my crossed arms, when Henry found me.

"Miz Lizzy!"

"Henry!"

I fell into his embrace, not caring he was a man of color, only knowing that he represented home and safety. He held me close to his big bear of a body, letting me cry like a baby, like the coward I was.

"You escaped," he said. "Thanks be to God."

I nodded, letting him believe the lie.

"Miz Grace?"

"In there," I said, my voice cracking.

"Lord, have mercy."

Henry released me and turned to stare at the rubble. The two men emerged with one body. Then two. Henry left me to help them. They brought out a little girl who was alive. It wasn't Grace.

Policemen and other citizens quickly descended upon the scene. They shoved me aside behind a hastily erected barrier. As a woman, I couldn't help, but only stand there helplessly as hour after hour dragged by. Distraught parents joined me, but policemen kept them back as well. All of us feared the worst, but hoped for the best.

People thought I'd escaped the cyclone that had destroyed the building. My clothes were torn, my face scared and bloody. I neither confirmed nor denied their assumptions. Living with my shame, a cold wound began to fester in my heart. An oozing sore I knew I'd live with the rest of my life

Horses-drawn carts were brought in to carry the dead to the city morgue or to temporary ones in nearby houses or saloons, anything that remained intact. The living were treated in nearby houses or offices. I marveled how the buildings across the street stood as dark sentinels to the whims of the chaotic winds of the cyclone.

Bodies were found in the hallways and stairs at the rear of the building. I remember Bob saying the back doors had been locked. The victims didn't know that and had run toward them in their panic.

Every time a person was brought out alive from the ruins, we cheered. If the person was dead, we strained to identify him. Was he or she our loved one? Many of the corpses were unrecognizable.

As the night progressed, I despaired even more of finding Grace alive. The top two stories had pancaked down upon the first where she had been learning to dance. The rescuers reached the area of the dance class someone said around 11:30. More bodies were removed. One by one, my fears were magnified.

And then Nurse stood beside me. She touched my torn sleeve. "Lizzy, you're alive."

I turned and saw her, barely registering her face in my shock. I nodded. There was truth in her statement.

"Grace?"

I shrugged. How could I know? I had deserted her and was nowhere near her when the cyclone crushed the building.

"I brought her coat. It's so cold," Nurse said, holding out a small black, wool coat for me to see. "I didn't think to bring yours."

She was almost apologizing to me. How strange.

I found my tongue. "Henry is in there." I nodded toward the rubble. "He's searching for her."

"Thank the Lord." Nurse lifted a gloved fist to her lips and held it there, as if she could prevent the cry of heartache she felt.

"Henry will find her," I said with an odd knowing. "He will bring Grace home."

Slow minutes crawled by. I felt no comfort in Nurse's presence because I feared she'd discover the truth. I'd shirked my responsibilities. I'd abandoned a child to perhaps die alone.

Our worst fears were confirmed around midnight. Henry emerged from the building carrying a lifeless form dressed in white.

"Grace!" I cried.

"Henry! Is she...?" Nurse couldn't finish her question.

The colored man marched up to us stoically, holding the limp body to him as if to protect her. He was a tall man and looked down at us with his face grim and eyes moist with tears.

"I found her, Miz Abigail," he said in his deep Southern voice. "She looks right at peace."

"Oh, dear God!" Nurse wailed.

I wept. A policeman let us cross the barrier and go to Henry and Grace. We wrapped the coat around her. The policeman offered to find us a cart to take Grace home.

"I'll carry her, if you please, sir," Henry said with a quiet dignity. "Mr. Chadwick gave her to me to protect. I s'pect I can see her home myself. She's just a little slip of a girl."

The three of us walked home. Henry in front, carrying Grace's body, Nurse and me in step behind, like a military parade. We didn't talk all that long way home as we passed businesses with their top floors missing or their fronts sheared away. Fallen bricks, broken glass, and toppled trees were everywhere. Snapped telegraph poles lay on the ground entangled with wire.

Once we turned onto Third Avenue with its tall mansions, we

left the horrible scenes of destruction behind. I could hardly walk. I was like a person drugged and sightless, simply reacting, not thinking or feeling.

How could I let myself feel? For to feel would mean I'd be overcome by grief so soul wrenching that it would be impossible to bear.

I endured like this, quietly, suppressing my emotions, through little Grace's wake in the morning room of the mansion. She was laid out on a table in her best Sunday dress, looking so peaceful and serene.

"She must have suffocated," Nurse said. "There's not a mark on her body."

I thanked God for that and prayed that she hadn't suffered long. I grieved in silence, but I deserved my isolation. In some respects, I welcomed it as penance for my wrong-headed behavior.

Grace's brother, Tom, came from Harvard for the funeral, but her parents couldn't sail from Southampton in time. We buried Grace on Palm Sunday, the first Sunday after the cyclone. A black-draped hearse and four black horses took her casket from the mansion to Cave Hill Cemetery. We went along too in a large open carriage. All the servants went, because we'd all loved Grace. It was fitting that those who loved her best were there to say good-bye.

When we turned to leave the gravesite, Henry remained. I walked with the others across the grassy slope to the carriage and heard Henry's clear bass voice singing, "*There is a balm in Gilead, To make the wounded whole; There is a balm in Gilead, To heal the sin-sick soul.*"

Six weeks later, when I learned I was pregnant, I sought out Grace's grave again, walking all the way to Cave Hill. It was a sunny May day with hardly a cloud in the sky. A gentle wind touched the leaves of the trees over my head. I sank down on my knees next to the newly turned dirt. I couldn't pray. Dry-eyed, I simply stared at the spot where Miss Grace had been laid for the final time.

"They found Bob Torrance's body in a saloon on Main Street that was next to the Louisville Hotel," I told the cold ground beneath me. "Bob must have gone there after he left me. Part of the hotel fell on the saloon, crushing the barroom patrons. It was a fitting end for him, don't you think?

Nothing. No answer. What did I expect?

"It should have been me," I said. "I should have been there with you, but you sent me away, didn't you? Did you know what was to happen?"

But how could she know about the cyclone? And how could a little girl know about the cruelty of a Bob Torrance and my own naiveté?

No, Grace didn't know what was going to happen, any more than I did. We couldn't see into the future. But I was the one who'd choose to shirk my responsibility. I was alive but would live with my shame the rest of my life.

When I finally climbed to my feet and dusted off my skit, I turned to find Henry watching me from a nearby tree. His eyes were dark with sympathy and something else I dared not try to comprehend.

He walked me home.

CHAPTER TWENTY-TWO

December 30, Present Day

I opened my eyes slowly. The remnants of a very vivid, terrifying dream floated on the peripheral of my consciousness. I was lying on my back and unable to move because of the cold seeping into my bones. But how could I be cold. Wasn't it just summer?

I let my eyes adjust to the darkness around me. *Where was I?* My hands were folded over my belly. I moved my right one and touched the hard canvas beneath my body. Something told me I was lying on an old World War II Army cot. How I knew that I didn't know.

What had happened to me? I was stiff and uncomfortable. Subconsciously, I reached for the antique locket that had belonged to my birth mother, forgetting I'd lost it.

It was there! Around my neck, lying against the flesh of my throat and chest under my knit Henley shirt, I found my locket. I fingered it, wondering if it was real. Wondering how it had gotten there.

My mind was hazy, my thoughts slow. I felt sick to my stomach. It was the same feeling I'd had at the party, but not as intense.

The party.

Where was Corey? Where was I? This wasn't the house shared by college students where Corey and I had gone to party.

I swallowed. My breathing was shallow. Overhead a sharp glow came from a window that was wider than it was high. No one could ever climb through it, I thought, as I looked up at it many feet above me and at the tall brick walls surrounding me. That was where the coldness came from—the damp bricks, almost as if I was underground somewhere. A musty smell hung in the air, cloying, closing in on me. Looking to my left, I discovered I was in a corner up against another hard, brick wall.

Nobody puts Baby in a corner.

I recalled the words from the movie *Dirty Dancing* and shivered. An icy fear replaced the confusion I felt. This wasn't right. I shouldn't be lying in what appeared to be an unused cellar. The last thing I remembered was feeling sick in the bathroom after the game of whatever it was called—that beer drinking game.

Eric!

And then I heard a woman's voice so clear in my head that the person could have been in the room with me.

Help yourself. Save yourself!

My eyelashes fluttered. I took another deep breath. A rosy haze appeared over my head and the face of a woman materialized. She smiled at me. She was beautiful with long blond hair and piercing blue eyes. She looked like me. Or did I look like her?

Melissa!

And then the words resounded in my head even louder. There was a pleading look in the eyes of the spirit or ghost or whatever it was that I was seeing.

Get up. Save yourself. Lock the door.

I pushed myself upright on my elbow and stared toward the end of the dark tomb of a room. At the far end was a door. Shut tight, it seemed. I struggled to sit up.

Get up. Save yourself. Lock the door.

I climbed slowly to my feet and then staggered toward the door, falling against it. I felt more than saw a gritty, iron bolt. I shoved it in place, securing the door, I hoped, as I had been instructed to do.

Then, my heart beating a mile a minute, I stumbled back to the cot and sat down.

I waited for what was to happen next. The vision had vanished with my movement. An unfathomable loneliness overcame me. That and a profound shame.

As I sat there, the images of my dream slowly seeped back into my consciousness. Now I knew how Grace had died. How she'd become a ghost. That woman Lizzy had left little Grace to face her death by herself. The poor child had probably been terrified when the floors above the dance hall and the walls around her had collapsed.

It didn't seem right. The loss of the child's life seemed such a waste. I mourned Grace's passing, thinking about her and the horrible dream I'd experienced more than my circumstances at the moment.

Somehow, I felt much safer because I'd thrown the bolt across the door. I had a measure of control over my situation. At least, I guessed I did. Because what control do any of us actually have over our lives? Over what happens to us? It's an illusion that we can control our lives, isn't it?

Moments later I heard footsteps outside. Then someone tried to open the door. It didn't give. Someone pounded on it.

"You bitch!"

Eric.

"Open the door, you bitch!"

I sat there frozen. A deep, abiding fear seared my gut. Eric was the reason I had been so sick. That I was isolated in this place wherever I was. He'd done this to me. Kidnapped me. Lured me away from the party. My mind was fuzzy with details. Now I remembered going with him. That was all. That and the dark nightmare of my dream.

"You let me in there, Beth. Do you hear me?"

I stood and ran to the door, placing my hands and right ear up against it, my heart thumping wildly in my chest. He couldn't force it open, could he?

"I won't hurt you," he was saying, softer now with a coaxing tone to his voice. "I promised to take you home. Open the door and let me in. I'll take you to your apartment."

The ridiculous words of the fairy tale "The Three Little Pigs" echoed in my head, "No, no, not by the hair on my chinny-chin-chin."

I didn't say anything, but expected Eric to answer, "Then I'll huff, and I'll puff, and I'll blow your house in."

Instead, he slapped the other side of the door with the palm of his hand. The door was strong and didn't budge.

"Damn you! Damn you, bitch, all to hell!"

Terror struck my heart. I trembled. My mouth was dry.

And then I heard another voice.

"What are you doing here, Eric?"

Jeff!

"Where's Beth? What have you done with her?"

"That's for me to know and you to find out," Eric replied in a challenging tone.

What happened next was hard for me to discern through the locked door. It sounded like a fistfight—as if I'd ever heard or seen one. But I'd seen enough of them on television, and my imagination ran wild. Long moments past as the pounding and thumping noise increased. My heart leapt to my throat. I was sick with fear.

And then I heard the gunshot. I'm guessing that's what it was since it was a crisp pop-pop that sounded nearby—menacing and dangerous.

"Oomph!" Someone grunted and hit the floor.

I heard sounds of running feet.

"Jeff!"

Not thinking about my safety, I wrestled with the bolt and unlocked the door. I threw it open and darted into a dark hallway. Jeff was crumpled on the floor against the wall. He was doubled over holding his belly. Had he been shot?

"Jeff!" I screamed, running to him and kneeling down beside him.

"Are you all right?" he asked, looking up at me. His face was bruised and bloodied.

"Yes, I think so," I replied. Gripping his upper arms, I searched Jeff's blue eyes fringed with long eyelashes. My fingers bit into the fabric of his red, wool sweater. "What about you? Did he shoot you?"

"He tried, the scalawag. The boy's no good."

Where had I heard those words before?

"I heard shots," I said and felt the pressure of unshed tears in my eyes. "I thought he'd shot you."

Jeff pulled me into his arms, cradling me, and we sat there hugging each other on the cold, brick floor. I started to cry as relief rushed through me like spring rain.

"I told you I have one or two guardian angels," Jeff whispered into my hair. He rested his chin on my head. "They saved me, telling me to dodge just the right way at the right time."

"Oh, thank God! My love, I was so worried about you."

He rocked me back and forth not speaking. But I thought I heard in my head an old Negro spiritual. "*There is a balm in Gilead, To make the wounded whole; There is a balm in Gilead, To heal the sin-sick soul.*"

After a few moments, Jeff asked, "Beth, did Eric hurt you?"

"I don't think so."

"Are you sure?"

I let out a breath, confused by the visions in my dream and the reality around me. "I don't know," I finally admitted. I reached for my locket, but it was gone.

Jeff squeezed me. "Corey and I think he slipped you a drug."

"A drug?" My mind was hazy.

"It's sometimes called a 'date rape drug'," he said.

"Oh, God!" I shuddered in his arms. "I don't know, Jeff. I don't know what happened to me," I wailed. "I don't remember a thing."

He sighed. "Dear God. Beth, we have to report this. We'll call the police and alert them to find Eric, because he's dangerous. And you need to go to the hospital."

"Why?" Fear roiled in my stomach. "I don't want to go to the hospital."

"You need to know if he raped you, Beth."

Jeff's words struck my heart with horror. I didn't feel like Eric had touched me. Only in my vivid memories of the dream did I sense the terrors of what an evil man could do to a woman.

Removing his iPhone from his shirt pocket, Jeff punched in 911. He gave a brief description of what had happened to us. He repeated it calmly as if he was very much in control. Then he gave the street address.

We were sitting in the basement of the Chadwick Bed and Breakfast.

CHAPTER TWENTY-THREE

A Louisville EMS ambulance drove me to a downtown hospital. Jeff rode with me in the back. The police had taken both our statements. Of course, I didn't have anything to report other than feeling sick and leaving the party with Eric. I was careful not to mix up my account with my visions of the house servant from so long ago.

If I thought not remembering was a nightmare, I was wrong. In the emergency room, I was probed and prodded and made to pee into a cup. A nurse took my clothing and put it into a bag. I'm sure she would have taken Melissa's antique locket, if I'd still been wearing it.

I couldn't comprehend its disappearance, so I didn't try. Alternately shaking from the chill in the room and from the humiliation of my situation, I sat on an exam table in a white gown that fastened in the rear and bared my backside.

"I don't know what happened," I kept telling the medical staff. "I was out. Asleep, I guess."

And reliving another woman's rape. But of course, I couldn't say that.

Yet, I did have to admit to having consensual sex within the last twenty-four hours. Heck, was it really only yesterday morning that Jeff and I had made love? I didn't think of it as 'having sex.' To me, it was making love. But the beautiful moment seemed so long ago and was cheapened by the events of my kidnapping.

With the white hospital lights glaring down on me, I felt numb and out of sorts. I just wanted to go home.

Corey came from my apartment and brought me another pair of jeans and sweatshirt. She was with me when finally a counselor told me I'd not been raped.

"We found the drug rohypnol in your system," I was told. "But no evidence of rape."

"Thank, God!" Corey uttered.

I bit my lower lip and sat a moment taking in the information. "So that's why I felt sick and passed out?"

"Yes. And why you don't remember anything."

I nodded. "Can I go home?"

"Yes. You're free to go."

Corey walked with me into the waiting room. Jeff was there. He looked so cute with his tousled hair and a tiny bandage next to his eye. All I wanted to do was kiss it and make it better, but he had a somber look on his face almost as if he'd erected a barrier against me.

"I'm pressing charges against Eric for breaking and entering," he said with a single-minded tone to his voice.

I nodded again unable to speak because of a painful lump in my throat. Suddenly, I didn't care about Eric and what he'd done, or hadn't done, to me. "I want to go home," I said.

"The police may have questions for you."

My posture sagged and my chin quivered. Shame swamped over me like a tsunami. Shame for being gullible and going with Eric even though I was sick and residual shame for the servant girl from the past whose outcome had been far worse than mine.

"Jeff," Corey intervened. "Beth needs to go home and rest. Can't she talk to the police later?"

Jeff must have taken a good look at me then. "Yes, of course."

He draped an arm around my shoulder, and I leaned against him as we walked through the hospital corridors. I soon found myself in the front seat of Jeff's car. Corey had picked it up for him at the house when she picked up my clothes and driven it to the hospital.

We stopped at Corey's house and dropped her off. Jeff took me home, but wouldn't allow me to go to my apartment.

"You're staying with me," he said. "I'm not letting you out of my sight."

He let me shower before tucking me into his king-size bed and kissing me good night.

It was the middle of the afternoon, but I didn't care. I was so exhausted that I must have fallen asleep as soon as my head hit his pillow.

When I awoke and turned on my side, Jeff lay beside me fully clothed on top of the covers. He'd thrown his left arm over his eyes and his chest moved slowly.

I watched him, hardly blinking, and drinking in his profile. The love I had for him poured through my soul, enlightening me with a radiant energy that rippled through me.

"Dear God, I love him," I whispered.

He moved. Turning to face me, a smile on his lips, Jeff let his left arm stretch out to pull me to him. It felt so good. So right. As if I belonged. As if I'd come home.

All my fears and insecurities pranced before my eyes, playing games with my senses. Did this man, this older man, love me?

Without my inheritance, I was nothing. Had nothing. Accomplished nothing. Why would he want me?

There was no rational explanation. But isn't that the way love is? We don't pick who we love. Or who loves us. It just sort of happens. As if it was some sort of cosmic ballet and we were the dancers.

"We've slept this way before," he said in a sleep-roughened voice.

"Yes," I whispered, thinking of the other night when I'd stayed over, and we'd made love as if it was going out of style.

"No," he said as if he read my mind. "Before this. A long time ago."

He was drowsy. Still sleepy. I snuggled nearer to him and let him cuddle me, enjoying the rush of security I felt.

And the profound feeling of belonging at last.

CHAPTER TWENTY-FOUR

July 1890
The Carriage House

The night after Henry walked me home, I crept downstairs to the little room behind the stables where he slept on a hard straw pallet. I crawled in bed beside him, fully clothed.

"What's you doin', Miz Lizzy? We'll get in trouble."

"I don't care," I'd told him. "I'm scared and sad. I have nobody else."

That had been enough for Henry at the time, and we'd continued meeting secretly like that for over a month. He didn't touch me physically in any way. We just shared a bed together, and I drew strength and comfort from his human presence. His strong energy.

But my life was about to change, and I didn't want to leave the Chadwick Mansion. I didn't want to leave Henry. With a baby growing in my belly, I had no choice. Strangely, it was Miss Abigail Smith who'd come to my rescue. Nurse, of all people, had shown a measure of compassion for my circumstances for I'd confided in her that I'd been raped.

Oh, I never admitted when it had happened—that it been the night of the cyclone, the night we lost Miss Grace. She thought it'd happened a month later than that, because I'd hidden my pregnancy until I told her.

But now, being about four months along, my belly was rounding. It wouldn't be long before I wouldn't be able to hide my condition.

Mr. and Mrs. Chadwick came home, sick with grief. Mrs. Chadwick appeared gray and drawn. She'd taken one look at Grace's empty room and swooned to the floor. Henry carried her to her bedroom where she'd stayed for days with dark, shrouded windows. I saw her in there grasping a locket, crying, her heart broken. I saw her take Grace's tiny photo out of the locket and lay it on top of a stack of other photos. She tossed all the photos of Grace into the fireplace, and then asked me to set them on fire.

I came away filled with my own grief and shame so heavy that it weighed on my heart.

After removing Grace's oil portrait from the library wall and placing it in the cellar at his wife's request, Mr. Chadwick questioned Nurse about the cyclone. I spoke in her defense, saying Nurse had been ill, and I'd agreed to chaperone Grace. Not the truth that I'd been ordered to do so or that it was Nurse's normal behavior when they were away.

Without a daughter to supervisor and instruct, the Chadwick's no longer needed Nurse's services. They let her go, but allowed her to stay until she found another position. She found one in Chicago where she had a sister who ran a boarding house and agreed to take me with her. I could help her sister, and as a "widow" give birth to my baby in a city where I was not known.

My baby. I didn't want Bob Torrance's baby—conceived so cruelly on the dreadful night that Grace died. My humiliation was palpable, coloring my attitude, ruining my formerly happy disposition, and sucking the life from my body even as a new life grew inside it.

My only salvation was Henry.

He learned about my condition but didn't judge me. Somehow he guessed when it had happened. We didn't talk about it, but the fact I'd escaped the Falls City Hall and Grace had not revealed more to him than I knew. After all, he'd seen the destruction whereas others had not.

On the night before Nurse and I were to leave, I sneaked downstairs one last time. Henry was awake, a lone candle burning on his only table. The quiet rustling of horses in their stalls and the night breeze were the only sounds. An earthy smell of hay and sawdust and horses permeated his tiny room. I associated those sounds and smells with Henry. Standing on the threshold, looking inside at him sitting on his cane chair, I pressed the memory of him into my mind.

I'd grown to love him—the big, burly black man with so much heart and compassion. And I dreamed that he loved me too. It was a different love from that silly infatuation I'd had for Bob. This was a connection that I couldn't explain. It was if it was meant to be.

"I want you to marry me," I said to him.

He looked up, startled. His jaw dropped.

"I want you to marry me and help me raise this baby."

"You know that's not gonna happen, Miz Lizzy." He shook his head, his dark eyes anguished. "You know there's laws against it. I can be put in jail. Even doing what we are doing can get me in trouble."

I entered the room and kneeled down beside him, my skirt bunching up around me. Taking his big, right hand in mine, I pleaded, "Maybe we can go up North or to California. Maybe to France. There's got to be some place where people like us can marry."

"You know we don't have any money for that kind of travel."

His practical words drew me up short. Henry was right. That was the reality of our situation. I had no hope of making a life with the one man who'd been kind to me. The one man who truly loved me.

He did, didn't he? I'd seen it in his eyes, but he'd never told me. Granted, I'd never told him. There hadn't been a need until now. It was just something that I'd accepted. As if it was the truth.

I let out a breath, fighting with my emotions. "You're right, of course."

"You know it too, in your heart."

His deep voice brought me no comfort. I knew when I left Louisville I'd never see him again.

"You know I love you, Henry," I said quietly.

"No! Don't say it. That's not right. It can get us in trouble."

"I don't care what other people think. It is *too* right. You know it just as I know it."

He turned his gaze away staring at the flickering candle.

"Tell me you love me, Henry," I begged. "At least let me take that with me."

Turning back to look at me, Henry's eyes were damp with unshed tears. "I'm ashamed I can't marry you, but it's too much to risk. I won't do that to you. Not in this day and age."

Henry lifted his chin as if to survey the darkened stable beyond the open door. "Maybe someday things will change and people like us can marry." He covered our hands with his left one. "Maybe our love can someday be acknowledged."

"You do love me!" I cried and bent my head to kiss his hands.

"I love you, Miz Lizzy," he said simply. "It grieves my heart that I can't do more than give you the words."

"No!" I raised my gaze to meet his. "It's enough. I can live with those words. I can live with them—until we meet again."

CHAPTER TWENTY-FIVE

December 31, Present Day

Once more I awoke in Jeff's bed, last night's dream vivid in my mind. Jeff was not there with me. When I looked at the alarm clock, I knew he'd gone to make breakfast for the guests. This morning I didn't care and simply turned over on my other side and stared at the impression his body had made on the covers.

I must have fallen asleep again, this time dreamlessly. When I awoke again, Jeff was sitting on the edge of the bed. He gently touched my shoulder.

"How do you feel?"

I turned over and stared up at him. "Confused, but okay, otherwise."

"We need to talk, don't we?"

He was reading my mind again. "Yes," I said.

"Get up, and I'll make breakfast while you clean up."

I took another shower, as if that could help scrub my mind of all its questions. At least my body felt better, more like myself. I found some undergarments Jeff had left me. He must have been to my apartment. And then I put on his white, terrycloth bathrobe, bundled up like a cuddly bear.

Breakfast was special. Jeff had fixed blueberry pancakes and bacon. The heavenly smell of frying bacon infused his great room with a comfortable feeling. It felt like home. Like my mom Sue fixing breakfast for me as a child, taking special care to make me scrambled eggs, not the fried, sunny-side-up eggs that my father insisted she make.

"I suppose I'll have to tell my mom what happened," I said to Jeff, sliding onto a barstool.

"She knows," he replied.

"You called her?"

He turned with a quaint grin on his face and placed the breakfast plate on the countertop in front of me. "No, she told me where to find you."

"Oh, yeah." I picked up a piece of crisp bacon and studied him. I remembered my vision of Melissa from the mansion cellar. "Are you really a medium?"

"Not a very good one, I'm afraid."

His remark was self-deprecating. I chewed the bacon. "Why do you say that?"

"It wouldn't have taken me so long to figure things out, if I was better at it. If I'd been more trusting. Tried harder."

"Well, if you've figured things out, I wish you'd explain them to me," I said with a touch of anger.

"Finish your breakfast first."

We settled on the leather sofa with our own mugs of coffee. I cradled my cup, letting the aroma waft into my senses. For some reason, I was more attune to everything—light, sound, smell, even the soft touch of the cotton bathrobe that wrapped me in comfort.

"I'm confused," I told Jeff. "What happened to me with Eric was a nightmare, but I had trouble separating that reality from the dreams I've been having lately."

"What do you mean?"

I explained my dreams to him then. About the mansion in the nineteenth century, its servants, the tornado, and Grace. It took a long time, because I relived my dreams as I spoke, my body alternating between cold and hot. Jeff sat at one end of the sofa, a knee bent so he could turn and face me.

"I just don't know if those dreams are true. They seem so real, but I was out, drugged. I just don't understand."

Jeff scooted forward, set his coffee mug on the table, and leaned toward me. "They are real, Beth," he said quietly.

"What do you mean?"

"Those things you saw, they actually happened to you."

"What?"

"Sometimes when we dream, the rational, judgmental part of our mind is suspended," he said. "In this unconscious state, we're receptive to another dimension. The dimension of our souls."

I must have looked confused.

He sat back. An ethereal look crossed his face. "We are actually spirit living in a physical body," he explained. "We are electromagnetic beings, souls, who incarnate into a physical body in order to learn the lessons that life on earth can teach us."

"You're kidding, right?"

Jeff shook his head, dead serious. "I'm telling you what I've learned from my spirit guides and angels. From Melissa after she crossed over. Souls progress further on earth than anywhere else in the universe."

I sat there, eyes wide, mouth slack. He wasn't kidding. Jeff believed what he said. But the implications of what he said were too stunning to be understood.

"Souls incarnate as many times as necessary to attain their goals."

Attempting to comprehend, I held up my hand for him to pause. "You're talking about reincarnation."

"Yes."

I could see he was happy that I was getting it. But was I? Except for those few dreams recently, I remembered nothing about anything of a past life and told him so.

"We don't usually. It's like we have amnesia when we incarnate again in another body. The past life, or lives, are hidden from our consciousness. We're humans in a human body. Our memory of our soul life is suppressed."

Jeff reached for his mug of coffee and took a sip. Then he set it down again. He looked up at me and smiled.

"That's not to say we don't bring our issues with us from our past lives. They seem to replay over and over again until we work it out. Until we get it right."

A sharp intake of breath signaled my understanding. "Are you saying I was this Lizzy person? The girl I dreamed about?"

He nodded. "Yes."

"So I was responsible for Grace's death?"

He slowly moistened his lips. "No. What I'm saying is that the events of that time continue to affect your life today."

"Like what?"

"Melissa has shown me that the shame you feel today, your lack of self-esteem, is a direct correlation to what you felt in that time because of your actions then."

I sat back, gazing at him, absently rubbing my arms and trying to take it all in. "I just can't believe it."

"There's another concept about soul groups and soul families. How we incarnate time and time again with the same souls. How our lives play out separately, but together. On this earthly plain, we can run into souls who have been integral parts of our past lives."

I cleared my throat before asking, "So are you saying that I have known people in my life in other lives?"

"Yes."

"Have I known you?"

His eyes softened. "I've known we were connected since the moment we met."

The tingling in my chest surprised me. I acknowledged to myself that I'd had the same feelings. It was as if I'd known Jeff all my life. Or was it many lives?

My thoughts scrambling to make sense of it all, one thing was suddenly clear to me. "Are Eric and Bob the same soul?" I asked.

Looking toward the window, Jeff cocked his head as if listening. "Melissa says yes."

"Well, he hasn't learned anything has he?"

Jeff chuckled a little. "I'd say he's got a long way to go."

"What about you? Where did you show up?"

His eyes narrowed, as if daring me to speculate. He grinned. "Can't you guess?"

My heart did a little dance. "Henry?"

"I meditated last night while you slept. Although I felt our soul connection, I didn't know how. My spirit guides helped me understand. I saw everything from 1890 that you just explained to me, but from Henry's perspective."

"But he was a black man."

"We don't reincarnate in the same way. We can be a different race or gender with each incarnation."

"Oh, my God, Jeff." I sat back against the pillow. Warmth flowed from my heart throughout my body. "What happened to us?"

"Lizzy left and went to Chicago where she had a baby girl. Because of the miscegenation laws that enforced racial segregation, they couldn't marry or even have intimate contact. Lizzy raised the baby, but died of pneumonia when she was about forty."

"And you? Henry?"

Jeff shrugged. "Henry stayed at the mansion for the rest of his life, although the automobile put him out of a job. He died at a ripe old age, never marrying, and always ashamed that he could do nothing to help Lizzy."

Deep sadness and regret washed over me for the lives ruined and wasted, lives unfulfilled, and love unrequited.

More than that, I understood for the first time that the nagging guilt I'd always carried came from Beth's life as much as from the wrong-headed choices in my current one.

"Aren't you glad for a second chance?" Jeff asked, as if he'd read my mind.

"Oh, Jeff." I reached for him. He caught my hand in his, and in some strange respect his grip reminded me of Henry's strong one. "And you're still protecting me today," I observed.

"Maybe this time I can do it right."

Yet, there was one soul who never had a second chance, Grace. She still inhabited the earth plane as a ghost, her soul refusing to go home. I'd been the reason she'd died alone possibly terrified. Maybe I could help her home. With Jeff's help, of course. I knew I couldn't do it alone.

"You have to help me," I said, the tone of my voice rough with urgency. "You can't say no, and this time you won't fail."

Jeff gazed into my heart. He knew and nodded his head.

"Tonight," he said, "we will send Grace into the light."

CHAPTER TWENTY-SIX

New Year's Eve, Present Day

Jeff had a job to do at the bed and breakfast. One of the new guests had booked the front rooms and dining room for a small New Year's Eve party. Corey was coming over to work, but he could use my help as well. When he left the apartment for the big house, I went upstairs to change clothes.

My apartment was just as I'd left it except for the closet door standing open where Corey had picked out the clothes to bring to the hospital. I took a deep, satisfied breath, glad to be home. For once, I had no desire to be anywhere else. My future would surely turn out differently now that I understood. Oh, I didn't have the verbal assurance of Jeff's love, just an intense "knowing" that clad my heart with happiness.

I took my time dressing, choosing gray wool pants and a turquoise blouse. When I opened the dresser drawer to search for a pair of earrings for my pierced ears, I saw it.

Turning my head away, I covered my mouth with a hand. When I looked back, it was still there tucked in among my other few pieces of jewelry. The antique locket glowed with an otherworldly light. I reached into the drawer and picked it up. My fingers tingled.

"Thank you," I said out loud to Melissa.

I was talking to the spirit of my dead birth mother, but it didn't seem strange. Instead, a rush of euphoria rocked my senses. I felt alive and whole for the first time in my life.

"Don't take it away again," I warned. "I promise I won't lose it this time."

I clasped the locket around my neck, smiling at nothing, and wore it when I went downstairs to join Jeff and Corey.

Near midnight, the party going strong, Jeff brought me a glass of champagne. "Corey is going to watch the party for us in case the guests need anything. Let's go celebrate on our own," he said.

I took the fluted glass from his hand and let him lead me to the library, which had been shut off, the door locked for the evening. Jeff unlocked it and drew me inside. The room was chilly. The security light from the courtyard glowed through the curtained window, the same light I'd seen when locked in the cellar downstairs.

Jeff placed his glass on the mantle near Grace's portrait and lit several candles until the room was illuminated as it had been before the advent of gas lamps and electricity. There was a soft radiance in the library along with the comforting smell of the lavender candles and leather books. Picking up his glass, Jeff turned to me and raised it in a toast.

"Have I told you lately that I love you?" He had a silly grin on his face.

My pulse raced. "I believe Henry told Lizzy."

"But I haven't told you?"

"No."

He took a step nearer. The grandfather clock in the hall bonged the hour. "It's midnight. A new year. Drink with me, Beth."

We sipped the champagne, watching each other over the rims of our glasses. Electricity sparked between us. Then he lifted the glass from my hands, put both glasses down on a table, and turned back to me. The last of the twelve bongs sounded.

"Happy New Year, my love."

Jeff pulled me into his arms, and we kissed. I thought I'd drown in his embrace. He could sweep me away, and I wouldn't care.

"I love you, Beth."

"Oh, dear God, Jeff. I love you too."

At that moment, I heard the laughter. It wasn't an evil laugh, but a giggle full of joy and happiness. I pulled back from Jeff and turned my gaze toward the portrait over the mantle.

"Grace!"

A silver light flickered over Grace's portrait and soon the figure of a little girl with long, dark blond ringlets and a white frilly dress materialized in front of the fireplace.

The locket at my throat seemed to vibrate. Breathless, my adrenaline rushing, I took a step toward the vision of the child. She opened up her arms. I dropped my arms to my sides, facing my palms out toward her in a motion of supplication. I wanted to see her run to me as she'd done many times before, back when I was a lowly servant girl and she was the beloved, only daughter.

I took another step toward the fireplace. "Grace, I should never have left you alone. I'm so sorry."

In my head, I heard the words, "It's not your fault."

Jeff stepped up beside me. I glanced to my side at his upturned face. His eyes were shining, as if he too saw little Grace. Wasn't he only clairaudient? I thought he couldn't see spirits.

"She's telling you to forgive yourself," Jeff said in a quiet voice.

"She wants you to know there's no shame in being raped. It wasn't your fault."

"But I shouldn't have left her alone to die!"

Jeff nodded. "Okay, I'll tell her." He looked at me. "She says it was her time to go, but not yours. She sent you away so that you'd be safe. But she didn't know what Bob was going to do to you. We all have free will."

I trembled. My knees felt as if they'd buckle beneath me. "Oh, Grace!" I cried out.

Jeff drew in a deep breath and then released it. "Yes, I understand," he said toward the hovering white light. "Beth, she says that you were the only person who played with her and paid her attention. She loved you for it. When you blamed yourself so much, she knew she needed to stay around to make sure you understood about forgiveness. About love."

"But Lizzy left town." Quiet tears spilled down my cheeks. "You couldn't follow me, Grace, and I never returned."

"She waited for you all these years, Beth." Jeff's statement held the ring of truth.

"Thank you," I whispered, becoming suddenly still. "But you must go home. To heaven. Grace. It's time for you to go into the light."

The white form flickered. "Help her, Jeff," I begged.

When I glanced up, Jeff's eyes were shut as if he was praying. Then he opened them, and said in a low voice, "Grace, there are people in the spirit world waiting for you. Your mother has waited for you for a long time. She wants you to join her."

"Go," I said. "You don't belong here, Grace. I'm okay. I love you. I understand why you stayed and want you to go home."

"It's okay," Jeff said quietly. "They're waiting for you on the other side."

I reached for Jeff's hand. In the moment that we touched, the vibrating light vanished. The room warmed.

"It's done," I said with a sigh. A sense of peace descended in the room. "Thank you for helping Grace."

Jeff pulled me into his arms. "It's you I need to thank. You believed in me. You gave me confidence to explore my spiritual gifts."

I gazed up into his eyes, my stomach fluttering, feeling safe and whole.

"You're no longer scared about what you'll find?" I asked remembering that he said he'd been afraid.

"Not anymore." He kissed my forehead as I leaned against him. "Because what I found was you, Beth Abbott. And this time, we can be together for an eternity."

THE END

ABOUT JAN SCARBROUGH

Jan Scarbrough is the author of the popular Bluegrass Reunion series, writing heartwarming contemporary romances about home and family, single moms and children, and if the plot allows, about another passion—horses. Living in the horse country of Kentucky makes it easy for Jan to add small town, Southern charm to her books and the excitement of a horse race or a big-time, competitive horse show.

Leaving her contemporary voice behind, Jan's *My Lord Raven* is a medieval story of honor and betrayal. In *Freely Given* she collects short romances about women attempting to preserve their autonomy in the Middle Ages. Her paranormal Gothic romance, *Tangled Memories*, is a Romance Writers of America (RWA) Golden Heart finalist. *Timeless* is her latest Gothic romance.

A member of Novelist, Inc., Jan has published with Kensington, Five Star, ImaJinn Books, Resplendence Publishing, and Turquoise Morning Press.

Visit Jan at her website and on Facebook. You can also follow Jan on Twitter.

If you enjoyed Jan Scarbrough's *Timeless*,
please consider telling others and writing a review
on sites such as Amazon and Goodreads.

You might also enjoy these Gothic and Medieval romances
by Jan Scarbrough

Tangled Memories
Will following her heart lead her to eternal love or to a nightmare that will never end?

Freely Given (short Medieval Romances)
Happily Ever After doesn't always start as a fairytale romance...

My Lord Raven
He was so powerful. The ultimate warrior. She was his quarry.

Read the first chapter!

Tangled Memories

Present Day

His eyes were gray. I had never noticed before. They weren't the color of slate, but smoky and mysterious.

Swallowing a hard knot of dread that surfaced in my throat, I walked down the silent aisle toward him. Chin held high, very lady-like in posture and demeanor, a trace of smile upon my lips— I was the picture of confidence.

Inside, I trembled.

I stopped in front of the altar. A cloying scent of gardenias assaulted my senses. How curious the delicate white flowers in my bouquet should be so over-powering. Just like the man beside me. Just like the deep, heady gray of his eyes.

I extended my hand. As he took it, I drew a breath and held it. The firmness of his fingers surprised me.

"Friends," the minister said, "we are gathered together in the sight of God to witness and bless the joining together of Mary and Alexander in Christian marriage."

Alex was tall, so tall I was forced to look up into those mesmer-izing eyes. My breathing started again—erratic and shallow. How ironic. I married again for the second time in my life, and for the second time, my reasons were more practical than romantic.

How even more ironic was the Methodist minister's white stole, symbol of purity and love. I felt neither pure, nor in love. His black robes better matched my somber mood.

"I ask you now," Reverend Watts said, "in the presence of God and these people, to declare your intention to enter into a union with one another."

To enter into a union.

Heaven help me. Would it be a union? How could it be? It was a business arrangement, plain and simple. I understood that. For some reason though, sadness clutched my heart.

Reverend Watts looked at me and smiled. "Mary, will you have Alexander to be your husband to live together in holy marriage? Will you love him, comfort him, honor and keep him, in sickness and in health, and forsaking all others, be faithful to him as long as you both shall live?"

My stomach churned. Alex's penetrating gaze burned upon my upturned face. "I will," I said at last.

"Alexander, will you have Mary to be your wife?"

From underneath my lashes, I watched him. He wore his black hair swept back and long, curling at his neck. A stray lock touched his forehead and set off his eyes. His high cheekbones and jawline gave him a classic look. His lips were full and inviting. Enigmatic in his formal black tuxedo, crisp white shirt and bow tie, he seemed a brooding Byronic hero. Handsome, though austere, his masculine good looks belonged to another century or at least on the cover of a romantic novel.

How different would my life have been if I hadn't become pregnant at eighteen...if I hadn't married Bill...if I hadn't miscarried? What if I had met Alexander Dominican under different circumstances, before life had touched me so cruelly?

"I will." His deep voice resonated throughout the empty chapel.

Turning from the minister to me, Alex's eyes brightened as his gaze captured mine. Out of habit, I licked my lips, but nothing eased my tension. The strain I felt surely communicated to the self-assured man who held my hand. Did he feel the hypocrisy of our oath? Or was he simply satisfied with a marriage of convenience?

Daring him with my stare, I narrowed my own eyes in challenge to his casual acceptance of our deceit before God. His black brow lifted to meet my taunt. He cocked his head to the side as if to tell me I could yet back out. I could walk away a single woman. Poor, but single.

I shifted my gaze, unable to continue our silent joust, knowing full well I couldn't back out. Bill's death had made my current situation untenable.

"Let us pray. Eternal God, creator and preserver of all life."

I bowed my head, but I couldn't shut my eyes. It didn't seem right. Nothing seemed right these last few weeks. Not since the dark-clad police officer had come to my door telling me my husband of eight years had been killed in a car accident.

Bill and I hadn't been lovers in the end. Or even in love. Oddly, ours had been a simple marriage of convenience because of the baby...the baby who died. Yet, we had made a compact and married before God. I had honored our agreement, much as I planned to honor my new one with this new man by my side.

When the prayer ended, the minister motioned us to face each other and join both our hands. I gave the bouquet to Gail, my maid of honor. She hesitated, then took it. I was able to accept Alex's free hand. The grip of his fingers transmitted tingling warmth through my arms. Trite as it sounds, I felt my heart skip a beat.

What was this reaction? It had been a long time since I'd felt sexual attraction, and I certainly did not expect to feel ardor toward this man with whom I had signed a contract. What good would my feelings do? Although married, we had an arrangement. Ours would be a platonic relationship. Because his wife Allison had died so suddenly, I would be a mother his infant daughter. He would pay my debts.

Why had I agreed to such a stark and precise agreement? It left no room for this unexpected play of emotion.

"I, Alexander, take you, Mary to be my wife."

To be my wife.

My throat constricted. I had met Dr. Alexander Dominican the night I had lost my baby. The partner of my regular OB-GYN Dr. Hilliard, Alex had been on call. Still regretting my teen years, I knew had been such a fool to let myself get pregnant.

Straightening my shoulders at the thought, I caught the slight narrowing of Alex's eyes, and turned self-consciously from his scrutiny. What did he really think about me? Did he remember that scared teen-patient of eight years ago? I had changed. At twenty-six, I was now a woman. Did he know that? Did he care?

The minister nodded. Summoning all my willpower, I repeated in a hushed voice the same vows. My hands were damp when Alex released them to turn to his best man Dr. Hilliard. At the same time, Gail handed me a thin gold band. Unable to meet Alex's gaze, I took his left hand and slid the band across his third finger.

A strange feeling of familiarity enveloped me. In a different time, I believed he would have bowed and kissed the back of my hand. Today, he held onto it, and gently slipped the new wedding band into place. I glanced up to find his eyes appraising me. As I tightened my lips, my returning gaze did not falter. The weight of the ornate, gold ring nudged into my flesh and created a symbolic link between us.

"Bless, O Lord, the giving of these rings, that they who wear them may live in your peace and continue in your favor all the days of their lives."

Alex smiled a slow, half smile, as if he understood something I failed to discern. The smile softened his stern features, bringing back my recollection of the gentle doctor who had once comforted and cared for me. I offered a smile in reply, and was gratified to see his eyes lighten in response.

The minister joined our hands together again and wrapped his white stole around them.

"Now that Alexander and Mary have given themselves to each other by solemn vows," he said, "with the joining of hands, and the giving and receiving of rings, I announce to you that they are husband and wife; in the name of the Father, and of the Son, and of the Holy Spirit. Those whom God has joined together, let no one put asunder."

A surprising disquiet pricked my scalp and traced down the back of my neck. I swallowed once, to ease the dryness in my mouth and then looked up from our joined hands. We were husband and wife. It seemed so appropriate, so right. As if it was meant to be. But how could it? Under the strained circumstances of our compact, we were nothing but business partners.

"Are you going to kiss the bride?" I heard amusement in the minister's voice. Did he expect us to be a conventional couple?

Alex released my hands. I felt oddly bereft. He stared at me, his eyes shadowed by coal-colored lashes. I read the speculation in them. He lifted his hands, and I fixed my gaze upon them, charmed by the beauty of his tapered fingers. His hands lingered in the air briefly, and then Alex raised the thin veil from my face. My gaze now held spellbound by his, I watched as he gently elevated my chin with a fingertip and caressed my cheek with a thumb.

For an instant, my heart hung suspended in my chest, then dropped into a relentless beat. Why did I welcome the touch of his hand upon my skin? Dreamily, I smiled.

He stood so very close. His warm breath touched my face. I saw the flecks of dark in the lighter gray of his eyes. My own eyes widened in dismay as Alex lowered his lips to mine, tenderly touching them with a kiss so poignant it pierced my soul.

The kiss startled us both. I could tell by the way he hesitated, seeming to gasp for breath. With his left hand, he caressed my face, connecting us to each other in an untold way. I found it hard to breathe. I found it hard to move. In the recesses of my mind, warning bells clamored.

I straightened my shoulders and shifted my chin away from his touch. We may be married, but his kiss was not appropriate for two people with a business arrangement. Awkwardly separating, we held each other's gazes an instant. I felt dazed, swaying from side to side. Alex set his jaw and glanced away.

"Congratulations." Reverend Watts pumped Alex's hand.

Gail gave me my bouquet and offered me a swift hug. Her face was strained, her lips pursed. "I hope you'll be happy, Mary."

"Thank you."

Holding on to Gail's hug longer than was necessary, I then stepped back, embarrassed. I knew she was upset with me for marrying Alex. My friend had tried to talk me out of it, especially so soon after Bill's death. My reasons were wrong she had told me. I was being purchased like a broodmare for the price of my late husband's gambling debt. A significant gambling debt, I had tried to remind her. Bill had owed more than three hundred thousand dollars that became my debt after his death. I had no other way out. Gail and I had argued. It was no surprise we now had so little to say to each other. We treated each other like birds ready to take flight.

Nearby, Dr. Hilliard congratulated Alex, slapping him on his back.

"How do you capture the pretty ones, my man?" Dr. Hilliard asked. "How do you do it? You've got a beauty here for a wife. I ought to know...." He finished his sentence with a meaningful wink.

I thought his remark crude. He was my gynecologist, after all, and of course *knew* me in a medical sense. But I overlooked it and allowed him to congratulate me with what I thought was to be the obligatory kiss for the bride.

It was more like a lover's kiss. His tongue invaded my mouth. He held me tightly with too much familiarity.

Tasting bourbon, I abruptly ended the kiss, tossing my head as if to fling the flush of outrage from my heated face.

"Why, Dr. Hilliard," I snapped. "You certainly have a knack for exploratory surgery. Did they teach you that in medical school?"

He laughed. "Yes, Alex, I love a woman with spunk."

"Or is it just *my* women you love, John?" My husband's tone was slick ice.

I tried to assess the undercurrents swirling around me, only to find Alex's stony demeanor unreadable.

Thankfully, Reverend Watts interrupted our conversation. "Please step into my office to sign the marriage certificate," he said, then led us out of the quiet sanctuary.

Alex took me possessively by the hand and tucked it under his arm. He kept hold of my fingers, his own hand warm and sure. I had no trouble keeping up with his deliberate pace. There was something strangely comfortable about the way our strides matched.

"He's been my doctor for eight years," I murmured, "but I never realized Dr. Hilliard could be so insufferable."

"You've only seen him on his best behavior at the office. My esteemed partner usually doesn't come to work under the influence of Maker's Mark."

"He's not an alcoholic, is he?" I asked, thinking about my late husband.

Alex paused and looked down at me. "Let's just say he's walking a fine line where I'm concerned. I've been monitoring his behavior. Oddly, his behavior has worsened in the past months since Allison's death."

I gave Alex a slight smile, grateful for his explanation.

"They are waiting," he remarked. "Let's go in."

The minister's office was hot. Summer sunshine strayed through open drapes. We crowded inside while Reverend Watts went to a window air conditioner unit and turned it on. A blast of cool air erupted into the room. Returning to his desk, the minister shuffled papers for what seemed an eternity, finally producing a formal-looking document. When he nodded at us, Alex released me and stepped forward. Standing slightly away from him, I watched my new husband bend over the minister's desk and put his signature on the paper.

My situation seemed so unreal. Gail was angry with me. My trusted doctor had a drinking problem, and I was married ... again ... to a man who mystified, but intrigued me.

Suddenly, a high-pitched ringing sound shrilled loudly in my ears, growing in intensity until it blocked out other sounds. Was something wrong with the air-conditioning unit? Alex turned toward me, offering me the pen. His mouth moved, but I couldn't hear him speak. The stuffy little office grew fuzzy. Sweat beaded on my upper lip. I felt so weightless—as if I was floating.

Like Fourth of July fireworks, pulsating lights of exploding colors shot before my eyes. I closed them. In the distance behind my eyes, I saw a young girl dressed in a strange yellow gown. The room vibrated....

THANK YOU!

For purchasing this book from
Saddle Horse Press